MOON

Rain McAlistair

Ireland 2012

Front & Back Cover Photography by Kit

ISBN - 13: 978-1478370949
ISBN – 10: 1478370947

This book is dedicated to Simon

"The sincere friends of this world are as ship lights in the stormiest of nights."

Giotto di Bondone

Also by Rain McAlistair

Dove (2010)

Bridge (2011)

CHAPTER 1

Indigo sat on the smooth wooden floor of her father's London flat, surrounded by papers and official letters. Paul Keane had led a very simple life and there wasn't much to sift through. Utility bills, flyers from local businesses and a handful of old lotto tickets made up the bulk of what had been in the drawer.

There wasn't a lot to show for his 47 years on this planet. In the far corner of the drawer, Indigo had found three guitar plectrums. She held them now in the palm of her hand, thinking how he must have held them. They were a deep blue tortoiseshell colour and shaped like teardrops.

The years rolled back in her mind and she was six years old again. That was the year before he had left. She saw herself snuggled up in her red and white duvet, lying on her side, smiling sleepily up at him. He sat on the end of her bed, handsome and strong, his guitar balanced on his knee as he strummed and sang very softly.

Sometimes we'll sigh
Sometimes we'll cry
And we'll know why
Just you and I
Know true love ways

His favourite song. He sang so many songs. Songs she loved; songs she knew every word to. But this one was his favourite and he always ended the night by singing it. It was her favourite too...

She wiped away a tear. The guitar case stood in the corner. She wouldn't open it yet. She wasn't ready. She could picture his guitar so clearly, even though she hadn't seen it for twenty years. The dark brown wood, lovingly polished despite the small chips and dents in the body. The cream coloured volume and tone controls. The ends of the strings that he never snipped off, sticking out at wild angles.

Most of all she remembered the moons. Ten of them, arranged all along the fingerboard. The moons that guided his hand to play the right chords. Other guitars had dots, she had learned that when she got older. But her dad's guitar was special. The last things she would see before she drifted off were the white crescent moons, her eyes closing as he sang her to sleep.

'How are you getting on, love?' Paul Keane's landlady, Mrs Pettigrew stood in the open doorway holding a green mug. 'I've just made a brew so I thought you might like a cup.' She came into the room and handed Indigo the tea. 'So sad that he was taken so young. He didn't talk much but I heard him playing his guitar and singing many a time down here.' Mrs Pettigrew lived in the flat above this one. She had given Indigo the key when Indigo knocked on Mrs Pettigrew's door an hour earlier.

Indigo's mother, Noleen had phoned Mrs Pettigrew on the instructions of Paul's friend, Carl who had been with Paul at the hospital when he died four days ago. Noleen told the landlady to expect Paul's daughter who was coming to sort out his affairs following the funeral. Indigo had flown over alone to attend the service. Indigo lived in the West of Ireland and Noleen lived on the south coast of Ireland, 180 miles away. The two women had not seen each other for five years. They had never been close.

Indigo had left home when she was eighteen and now shared a house with Gillian who was studying jewellery making at college. She and Gillian had been good friends for a while before they decided to rent a house together.

Had it really only been a few days since she had heard of his death? Indigo had driven home from her job in the book shop with nothing more on her mind than what she was going to watch on TV that night. She parked outside the small grey bungalow, went in and put the kettle on. Going to the fridge for milk she saw a note in Gillian's handwriting stuck onto the fridge with magnets.

Your mum rang. Says to call her back ASAP.

Indigo and her mum only spoke on the phone at Christmas so she knew right away that something was wrong. She abandoned the half made cup of tea and went to the phone.

'Hello Mum. I just got your message. Is anything wrong?'

'Hello. Yes, I'm afraid I've got some bad news. It's your father.'

'Is he ill, Mum?'

'I'm sorry, Indigo. He was ill. He had cancer. He died this morning.'

'Died?'

'Yes. I'm sorry. Are you sitting down? Is anyone there with you?'

'Was anyone with him?'

'Yes. A friend of his called Carl rang me to tell me.' There was a long pause. 'Are you still there Indigo?'

'Yes.' She took a deep breath. 'I'll sort out a flight to London. Was he still living there when he died?'

'Yes. This Carl bloke gave me the number of his landlady. I'll organize for you to go to his flat. Do you mind sorting out his things?'

'Aren't you going over, Mum? For the funeral, I mean?'

'No, he probably has a girlfriend. They won't want me there.'

After the call, Indigo walked through the house and went out into the garden. She sat on the bench there. It was autumn but warm for the time of year. She had worshipped him. He had been her hero. But he had left her. One morning when she was seven she woke up to find him gone. And that was it. He never came back. He never wrote. He never sent birthday or Christmas cards. He had simply gone out of her life forever. One minute she had a dad and the next she hadn't.

The night before he had gone he had sung her to sleep. She heard him sing *True Love Ways* for the last time. As she had grown older she had realised that he wasn't coming back. It didn't stop her heart from breaking every time she heard Buddy Holly sing it on the radio. Just like it was breaking now.

*

'Was it a nice service, love? Mrs Pettigrew was asking now.

'Yes,' Indigo lied. In truth, the priest had not known Paul and the funeral seemed as though it could have been anyone who was being buried.

'I'm glad he had a nice send off. Well, I'll leave you to it.' The landlady went back upstairs leaving Indigo alone in the silent room. She picked up her jacket and felt in the pocket. The envelope was still there.

At the funeral yesterday a tall man had come up to her. 'Are you Paul's daughter?' he asked. She said she was and the man introduced himself as Carl.

'I was a friend of your dad's.' he said. 'I went to see him in the hospital. He asked me to phone your mum and he asked me to write down a letter for you.' Carl looked a bit embarrassed, fumbled in his pocket and handed Indigo a small white envelope. 'He told me what to put. I just wrote it down. He was too ill to write by then, you see. The death certificate is in there too'

Indigo looked at him with surprise and took the envelope. She had it with her in her hotel room last night and this morning but for some reason she hadn't opened it. But now, as she heard Mrs Pettigrew shut the door upstairs she felt ready. She put all the papers back in the drawer first and walked over to the window. She put the three plectrums in her jeans back pocket and began reading.

My dear Indigo,

I'm so sorry the way things worked out. I couldn't stay. It was killing me. I'm sorry I wasn't a good father to you. I have thought about you over the years. I always told everyone about my beautiful daughter in Ireland. I hope your life is long and happy. Please don't think too badly of me. Look after my guitar. It's yours now.

All my love, Dad.

Indigo went to his wardrobe. His clothes were hanging up quite neatly. She saw a faded black leather jacket, took it down from its hanger and put it on. It was far too big for her. It had a strong leather smell but also the faint touch of a masculine aftershave smell. She put it back on the hanger.

She drank the tea and then walked over to the guitar case in the corner. She laid it down on the floor. It was surprisingly light. It had stickers all over it. They looked like souvenirs from countries her dad had been to. She flipped open the metal catches all round the case and taking a deep breath lifted the lid. The case was empty.

*

Mrs Pettigrew thought Paul's daughter was brave to come to London on her own under the circumstances. Of course she was a grown woman, probably in her mid twenties, but you'd think she'd have had someone to comfort and support her.

It was a most peculiar business. The mother had arrived at Mrs Pettigrew's door on Saturday. She was a dowdy looking woman who didn't smile much. She said she wanted to check over Paul's affairs but asked Mrs Pettigrew not to tell her daughter she had been there, because she was not intending to go to the funeral. 'I don't want my daughter to be upset, you see. It's awkward, as you can imagine when we've been split up for twenty years. He never kept in touch actually.'

That was the way of the world these days; families all messed up and kids growing up without fathers. Well, it wasn't anyone's business but theirs. Mrs Pettigrew went back to her ironing.

*

Back in her hotel room, Indigo's mobile phone rang. She had been lying on the bed with her eyes closed but not sleeping. The display said 'Clodagh.' Indigo and Clodagh had been dating on and off for about six months. They only lived 20 minutes away from each other.

'Hello?'

'Indi! What's going on? How are you? God I'm so sorry about your dad.'

'Thanks, Clodagh.' Indigo rolled onto her stomach.

'I've been ringing and leaving messages. I was so worried.'

'Sorry. I just needed some time to myself.'

'I heard about it all from Gillian. Is the funeral over?'

'Yeah, it was yesterday. I've just been to the flat.

'Oh you poor thing. Why didn't you tell me? I'd have come over there with you.'

'Clodagh, my phone battery is about to run out and I'm not sure where I put the charger. I'll call you later, okay?'

Clodagh sounded very uncertain. 'Oh okay then. Look after yourself, Indi. And call me soon.'

Indigo switched the phone off and sat on the edge of the bed. She wasn't thinking about Clodagh, she was thinking about the guitar. She so badly wanted to see it again. The white crescent moons were like magic symbols from her childhood.

She had asked the landlady when she returned the key if anybody had been in the flat lately besides herself. Mrs Pettigrew said that nobody had. It was a mystery. Somebody had obviously taken it. Why would someone take a guitar without its case? Maybe someone wanted it to look like the guitar was still there. After all, that's what she had assumed when she saw the case in the flat herself.

Was the guitar valuable? She didn't have any idea. It must be quite old, but was it from the 50s or 60s? If so, her dad must have bought it second hand, because he wasn't born until 1965. But he did love music from that era so this did seem feasible.

Suddenly she remembered her netbook that was in her bag. She fired it up and wondered for a while what she should type into the search engine. Finally she put 'electric guitar moon fingerboard.'

To Indigo's surprise, three different guitars came up. The first two had tiny moons on the fingerboard, showing the moon in different phases as you went up the neck. The moons were no bigger than the standard sized dots on any fingerboard. The moons on 'her' guitar were much larger.

The third guitar that came up in the search had large crescent moons, quite similar to what she remembered but they were red. The ones on her guitar were white. Also, the two guitars were completely different shapes to each other.

Indigo took a long, hot shower, dressed in fresh clothes and went down to dinner in the hotel restaurant. At the last minute, she had an idea and went instead to the bar for a before dinner drink. What she really had on her mind was to quiz the barman.

She asked for a glass of lager, which in Ireland means a half pint. Both her accent and her terminology pointed to her nationality.

'Ah! A fellow Irish person!' said the barman delightedly as he served her. 'Welcome to London. I'm Sean, from Dublin.'

Indigo introduced herself with a smile and got the usual query about her unusual name. 'My dad was a bit of a hippy,' she replied.

'Beautiful name,' said Sean. 'Are you here for the sight seeing?'

'Not really,' said Indigo. 'I'm looking to buy a guitar. Where would be the best place to start?'

Sean said, 'you can't go wrong if you start in Denmark Street. It's off the Tottenham Court Road. There's loads of music shops there. You'll be spoilt for choice!'

She chose gammon with pineapple and chips for dinner. She wasn't in the mood for anything fancy. After her meal she went up to her room and stood in the window for a long time, watching people go by on the street below. Lots of couples seemed to be walking hand in hand. She had never walked like that with anyone. She wasn't into public displays of affection, although some part of her envied these young lovers.

She wasn't in love with Clodagh. She had never been in love. She'd had her fair share of girlfriends but she had never lived with a girlfriend, or come close to being in a serious relationship.

She wondered if her father had loved her mother once, before he had left them. Indigo had always found her mother cold. Noleen never cuddled her or made much a fuss of her. Her dad had been fun. Once, he had taken her to the funfair and they had queued together to see the Wall of Death. She had been a bit scared in the crowds and had held his hand tightly.

They went up some steps and stood at the rim of a bowl shaped wooden chamber where a man on a motorbike had ridden round and round, coming closer and closer to the top. The rider kept looking as if he would fly off the track into the spectators and every time he steered towards the edge the crowd went 'whoo' and leaned backwards. Indigo had been scared but excited. She remembered the smell of the exhaust fumes coming from the bike and the confident, proud expression on the swarthy rider's face.

On the way back, her dad had bought her some candyfloss. She liked the sound of the generators by the tents and stalls. She had loved the feeling of walking through the crowds in the dark, tightly gripping her dad's hand, with grass underfoot and their breath coming out like steam. It was a nice memory to fall asleep to.

CHAPTER 2

Francine's new student was a complete beginner. This could be good in a way, because it meant there were no bad habits to correct. The student was Polish but she spoke very good English. Her disadvantage to learning the guitar successfully was that she had hands like bunches of sausages. Her fingers were very short and stubby. However, Elton John had mastered the piano with small squat fingers so who was she to cast doubts on her student's potential?

'E, A, D, G, B and E,' said Francine, pointing to each of the guitar strings.

'Why is the bottom one E as well?' asked the student, pointing to the top string.

'That's called the top string, because it's higher. It's two octaves apart from the bottom E. They are the same note, two octaves apart.' Francine cleared her throat and hummed a low E then a high E. 'Can you hear that they are the same note?' The student looked doubtful but said, 'yes.'

By the time the hour was up, the student was playing a very nice full G major chord and both teacher and pupil were pleased with the progress made.

Francine gave lessons in a small room lined with windows above a music shop in Denmark Street. She also worked part time in the shop which was called Harmonix.

All her friends called her Frankie. The only people who called her Francine were her own mother and Derek's parents, Bridie and Patrick. Derek was Frankie's fiancé. She had met Derek when she auditioned for his band, Candyhorse. Frankie played rhythm guitar and liked to sing backing vocals. The band consisted of Derek on drums, Richard on bass, Sarah on lead guitar and lead vocals and herself. They had a regular slot on Saturday nights in a pub in Camden called the Singing Kettle.

Derek was very tall - six feet four and a half, with dark, thick hair and a killer smile. He was a year younger than Frankie, who was twenty-three and petite with chestnut brown hair that she wore in a sort of messy feather cut. She was a strikingly good looking woman and they made a very handsome couple. Derek was very family oriented. His parents were originally from Ireland. Patrick was a builder who had worked his way up from nothing to a successful business. Bridie stayed at home, fussing over Derek's three sisters and two brothers. The baby of the family, Ronan was only seven.

Bridie and Patrick liked Frankie and had big plans for her and Derek. It would be the first wedding in the family. Bridie had completely taken over the plans and had announced that Derek's sisters Sinead, Siobhan and Maeve would be bridesmaids. Bridie had decided that the bridesmaids' dresses would be peach coloured and she had also picked the church. It had been decided that Frankie would convert to Catholicism, and soon she was due to start going to their priest for Instruction. Frankie didn't have strong feelings about her own religion, but she did feel strange being forced into someone else's.

Derek's parents wanted their son and future daughter in law to live in the same road as them and there had been big hints that help would be given to buy a house. It was all taken care of.

Last week, Bridie had insisted that Frankie attend the annual dinner dance of a firm of builder's merchants. Patrick had close business ties with them. She hadn't really wanted to go, but couldn't get out of it. She had turned up in good time wearing a very smart pair of trousers and an expensive blouse.

'Oh no, no, no! This won't do at all!' Bridie had exclaimed when she had seen Frankie. 'You have to wear a dress. You can't go to a dinner dance in trousers! It's too late to go home and change. You'll have to borrow one of Sinead's dresses.' Frankie had felt a bit like a shop mannequin as she was poured into the dress and Bridie and Sinead poked and prodded her to try to make it fit.

It had been a horrendous evening. Bridie kept forcing white wine on Frankie. She didn't like wine and wasn't used to it. It was incredibly warm in the dining hall. During the speeches after dinner, Frankie had suddenly felt faint. The ladies' loo was what seemed like miles away, past dozens of tables. She took a few deep breaths, stood up and managed to stagger to the toilets where she sat on the floor before passing out. Bridie had followed her and then made her feel even worse about it by saying that none of her girls had ever fainted.

Frankie felt a bit stifled by all of this. She was in no rush to get married but she was very fond of Derek and did love playing in the band with him. Bridie and Patrick didn't approve of the band. They said they could get Frankie a job in a department store, through a friend who was a manager there. But Bridie often joked that the job would only be for a short time, until there were little ones on the way. Derek still lived at home and worked for his Dad. He had a gorgeous car which had been given to him by his parents but he was often at their beck and call to drive his brothers and sisters around. Frankie sometimes worried about his lack of independence.

Whenever Frankie went to visit Derek in their very impressive, large home, the whole family would hang around, mostly staring at her and saying little. It was as if they had been told by Bridie to socialise with Frankie or else they'd be in trouble.

Derek had a very generous nature. He was always buying her expensive presents and gave her flowers quite frequently.

They had got engaged during the summer. Candyhorse had gone into a recording studio on the second and third of July. They were making a CD to hand out at gigs, just to promote future gigs. The studio was in the countryside in a beautiful location. That weekend was very sunny and hot. Afterwards they had taken the recordings to Richard's house. Richard opened a bottle of champagne as they played the songs for the first time on his music system. The songs sounded great and they were all in an excited mood.

'Here's to Candyhorse and long may she run!' Richard toasted, raising his glass. Derek had then stunned everyone by making a speech of his own.

'Before you all drink all your champagne, I have an announcement to make. Frankie...' He took her hand. 'You are the most beautiful woman alive and it would make me the happiest man on earth if...' he knelt on one knee. '...If you would do me the honour of becoming my wife. Will you marry me Frankie?' He whipped the ring out of his pocket and offered it up to her.

Frankie blushed and caught sight of Richard and Sarah exchanging astonished glances. There was only one thing she could say, really. She said yes. But it had felt very awkward. The wrong place and the wrong time. And she wasn't a hundred percent sure that she was ready for such a big step.

Their CD was a great success. They had sold quite a few copies by now. Frankie was the main songwriter in the band but Derek had been writing for a while now too and they had written a few songs together. He had the knack of taking an average sounding song, tweaking a few notes here and there and changing a bridge, and suddenly, they had a really great song. Richard came up with some wonderfully melodic bass lines. He had a Rickenbacker bass, which looked as well as sounded great, and had a fretless bass too. One day in a moment of wild abandon he had taken his precious black Fender precision bass to a guitar doctor and had the fingerboard completely replaced with an ebony one without frets. It had added so much to their sound.

Derek played keyboards as well as drums. He wasn't an accomplished pianist but he was a whizz at programming and very clever at getting sounds out of his keyboard. He used the keyboard to write songs. A lot of the songs he wrote on his own were obviously about Frankie.

Candyhorse had quite big following in the area. The same people came to their gigs every week, although there were always new faces in the crowd to add to their growing fan base. They didn't have aspirations to become pop stars. But they wanted to enjoy playing their own brand of music for as long as they could. It was a real buzz and they got paid quite well for doing it too. Frankie had a very specific guitar sound, a composite of her playing style, her guitar and her amp. She liked a lot of chorus, a lot of reverb and plenty of treble. It all added up to a bright but rich sound. She was very happy playing in the band.

Frankie had a flat off Camden High Road, near Camden Lock, so it was only a short bus ride home from work.

She was passionate about guitars. The one she played most in the band was dark red stained wood grain and had a neck that went straight through the body. She thought it was a very feminine guitar as it was quite light in weight and had beautiful contours. She enjoyed looking for interesting second hand guitars in the other shops in the road where she worked, also checking out pawn shops further afield.

It was with this in mind that she set off now as she left work. She was heading for a pawn shop not far from her home. The man who owned the shop, Sid, often took in guitars. Sid greeted her warmly. 'Hi Frankie, how's tricks?'

'Hiya Sid. Got anything new in I might be interested in?' She leaned on the counter.

'Matter of fact I've had a guitar in this weekend you might fancy. It's different and pretty classy.' He pointed to the display behind Frankie.

The guitar was sitting on a stand in between a garish green Les Paul copy and some type of Strat. The dark brown wood was highly polished but her eye was drawn to the fret board. She noticed that it had 24 frets like her own guitar but what caught and held the eye were the beautiful white crescent moon shaped mother of pearl inlays. There were ten in all. Two moons marked the twelfth fret. It really was quite stunning.

Her eyes went to the headstock. There was no manufacturer's name or model name either. It looked like an old guitar so the name might have rubbed off over time. She had never seen a guitar quite like it.

'Can I try it, Sid?' she asked.

'Sure. Go ahead.'

The strings were very old and dirty and made a nasty dull sound but she could still tell that the action was very low. She ran through a few of her favourite chord shapes. The guitar felt so right in her hands. What she would love to do was to lay it on the counter there and then and change the strings and then plug it into her Vox AC30 amplifier and see how it sounded. You could never guarantee that the electrics worked on these old guitars but things like that could be fixed. Neither of these things was possible, however in the pawn shop.

Frankie put the guitar back on its stand reluctantly and tried to act nonchalant. 'How much are you looking for it, Sid? It sounds bloody awful but it's pretty to look at.'

'You're supposed to plug it in to make it sound good.'

'Really?' she joked. 'Well I never!'

'I'm looking for 150 for it.'

Frankie scratched her head. She knew you had to act fast on these things. The truth was that she had fallen in love with the beautiful guitar already and wanted it badly. 150 quid wasn't a bad price.

'140, because I'll need to spend a tenner getting new strings.' She wasn't one to haggle all day.

'Well...' Sid pretended to think about it. Frankie gave him her best smile. 'Seeing as it's you, doll... DONE!' He slapped his hand down on the counter. Frankie's tummy flipped over. She really wanted to do a happy dance there and then in the shop. But she remained calm.

'Have you got a few bin bags I can wrap it in?' she asked.

She only had a few stops to go on the bus but felt as though she was carrying something very delicate. She was so glad to get home.

The first thing she did was to carefully unwrap the guitar and place it on her bed. 'You are gorgeous,' she breathed as she looked at it.

She then looked in a drawer and was pleased to see an unopened packet of strings there. She took these and a yellow duster back into the bedroom and placed a pillow under the neck of the guitar. Gently, she began to remove the first of the worn strings. She wiped down the neck as she replaced each string, one at a time. The machine heads worked beautifully.

When she had all the strings on, the guitar looked better. She tuned it carefully. She sat on the bed, placed it on her knee and ran through some chords again. 'Wow!' It felt really good. Carrying it into the other room, she went over to her amp and connected the guitar to it, selecting a very low volume. She played four chords very slowly and then smiled a big smile. The sound was wonderfully sweet. Today had been a very lucky day indeed.

After playing it for over an hour she had located three small problems. The jack plug socket was slightly loose, there was fret buzz at the fifth fret and the intonation was slightly out at the twelfth fret. These were minor problems and could all be put right by her friend Mark, who was a guitar doctor. Tomorrow was Wednesday so he would be working at his shop in Denmark Street. She would drop it in on her way to work.

CHAPTER 3

Indigo woke up in a more positive mood. It was Wednesday. Her hotel was in Victoria. She studied her map of London over breakfast in the room. She knew there were supposed to be lots of book shops in the Charing Cross Road. She loved books and, as she worked with them too she thought it might be a good idea to look at some of the book shops and get some ideas for Brian's shop. Brian Heneghan was her boss back in Ireland. She could take the tube to Leicester Square and walk up the Charing Cross Road visiting any book shops that took her fancy. This would lead her nicely onto Denmark Street where she could begin making enquiries about the guitar.

An hour later she found herself standing in the Charing Cross Road, at the Leicester Square end. The very first book shop she saw was called Golden Sun Books and had a rainbow flag on their sign above the door with the double Venus sign. Wow! She had stumbled upon a lesbian book shop right at the start of her explorations. Brian's shop did have a gay and lesbian section of sorts but it was very small. She pushed open the glass door and a bell jingled as she went in.

She hadn't known there were this many books in this genre. The lesbian literature section was vast and she found many of her old favourites there. She browsed for more than an hour, then saw the time and hurried out. She didn't go into any other book shops on her way up towards Denmark Street. She may have time to go into them another day. She didn't know exactly how long she was going to stay in London. But she made a mental note of the ones that looked interesting for future reference.

When she got to Denmark Street she realised that Sean, the barman had not been exaggerating when he had said she'd be spoilt for choice when it came to music shops in this street. There were so many of them she had no idea where to start. Even the cafés had guitar themes. Eventually, she picked a small shop to start with because a lot of the guitars in the window looked old.

Indigo went up to the counter. The shop, as she had expected was quite noisy, with more than one person trying out guitars at once through the line of amplifiers down the centre of the room. The assistant was a red haired stocky man who looked to be in his early twenties.

'Hi,' he said.

'Hello. Uh, I'm looking for a guitar but I don't actually know the make or the model.'

'Okaaaaaaaaaay,' the assistant said slowly with a smile as if he thought this was a bit of a tall order.

'Well, it's electric and it has three control knobs at the bottom end...' said Indigo.

'That could be any of ninety per cent of the guitars in here!'

Indigo was undeterred. 'It's brown polished wood; dark brown and the really unusual thing about it is that it has half moon shapes on the fingerboard.'

'Half moon shapes,' repeated the man. 'No I don't think I have anything like that in stock. Is it for yourself or somebody else?' He was getting ready to launch into his sales patter. He had lots of guitars in mind that she might like.

25

'I'm really just looking for that specific one,' said Indigo. 'I'll come back if I find out anymore about it. Thanks for your help.' She went out of the shop and on into the next one.

In the second shop, the assistant pulled out a catalogue from under the counter and showed her a picture of the guitar with the red moons that she had seen on the internet.

'No, sorry, that's not it,' said Indigo. 'The moons on the one I'm looking for are white.'

'Oh well,' he replied. 'Good luck with your search.'

A dozen shops later she decided it was time to eat something. She walked to Oxford Street and went into McDonalds. She had a plain burger with just ketchup on it, a large fries and a cup of tea. It was very welcome.

Indigo was tired of searching by now. She decided to get a taxi to her dad's old flat. She had a feeling that if someone had taken his guitar, then maybe they had taken other things too. How did you start to look for the absence of things that you didn't know were there in the first place?

She wondered if Carl had taken the guitar. That made no sense though. He didn't have to give her that letter. He could have just thrown it away and she'd have been none the wiser that her dad still had the moon guitar. Anyway, Carl had struck her as a good guy.

The taxi driver asked her if she was on holiday. Indigo just said yes. She didn't feel like talking about her dad to a stranger.

Mrs Pettigrew gave her the key and asked her if she was feeling any better. She said she was and went down and let herself in again. Everything looked the same.

She sat on the sofa and thought. Her hotel was expensive and she couldn't afford to stay there indefinitely trying to track down the guitar. If only she could use this flat as a base, she could arrange some time off work and stay in London for longer. Her dad must have a rent book somewhere. The rent may be paid until the end of the month for all she knew. Today was the fifth. That would give her twenty-five days.

She began searching for the rent book.

*

Mark arrived for work on his racing bike, carried it into the shop and stored it away in the back room. He ran his guitar doctor service from a very trendy little guitar shop in Denmark Street. Customers left their guitars in with Joe, the young lad who worked in the shop every day. Joe attached a docket with the customer's name and phone number and a brief description of what needed to be done. Mark always phoned the customer after a preliminary check of the guitar to discuss what he was going to do.

Today he had three guitars lined up waiting for him in the tiny store room. One was a Gibson 335 in a shaped hard case. Very nice. The second was a cream coloured Fender Mustang in a battered old flight case. The last guitar was in a padded acoustic guitar gig bag. He could tell from the feel of the bag that an electric guitar was inside. He unzipped the bag and laid the guitar on the bench in his workshop. The top of the bench was protected by a padded mat.

He let out a slow low whistle as he took in the dark brown body, the maple neck and the rosewood fingerboard with the crescent shaped mother of pearl moon inlays. A Moonchaser. The first one he'd ever seen. For a while he just looked. Then he glanced at the details on the docket, picked up the guitar and carried it over to his Fender Twin amp. 'Let's put you through your paces, girl,' he said and began to play.

He played the blues. He wasn't in a band. He liked to play alone. He had had hundreds of guitars pass through his hands in his line of work. He was forty-five and had been working on guitars most of his life. He seldom got excited about a guitar. But this one was really something.

The Moonchaser was a dream to play. The strings seemed to meet his fingers, as if they willed the notes to come to life. The neck pick up sounded sweet and pure and the bridge pick up had a bite that made the notes soar. Mark played for a full twenty minutes. It was one of the best guitars he had ever played. It had come from Frankie, the girl from Candyhorse. He envied her this beautiful instrument. There was scarcely anything wrong with it either. It just needed some minor adjustments - a tweak on the truss rod and maybe he'd need to file down one of the frets very slightly. The jack socket was a bit loose. That was no problem. He'd have this baby perfect in under an hour.

Mark phoned the mobile phone number on the docket.

'Hello?'

'Hi this is Mark from the guitar workshop. I'm phoning you about the Moonchaser.'

'Moonchaser?'

'Yeah, the guitar you brought in this morning.'

'Is that what it is? I've never heard of that name before.'

'Where did you get it?' Mark asked. 'Have you had it long?'

'No I picked it up yesterday in a pawn shop.'

'Did you shell out much for it?'

'Um, £140 quid. It's a nice guitar isn't it?'

'I'll say! Do you know how much these axes sell for these days?'

'No. How much?'

'Well it's worth about five grand.'

'You're kidding me!' Frankie sat down involuntarily. She was astounded. 'I had no idea, Mark. I just bought it because it felt nice to play, sounded great and I loved those moons on the fret board. Is it old then?'

'These guitars were only made in the one year. 1969. They were made by a small company called Avocet based in Texas, in the States. They produced handmade electric guitars. They used traditional craftsmanship but combined it with modern innovation. Well, modern for those times. Those pick ups are their own and the moons on the fingerboard were a design unique to Avocet. They only made a handful. I've never seen one in the flesh before but I've seen one in a catalogue of vintage guitars. They're generally accepted as being up there with the best. I wonder how it came to be in a pawn shop?'

'Your guess is as good as mine. So how is it?'

'Sweet as a nut. I'd give my left arm to own one of these. I'll have it ready for you by lunchtime.'

'Thanks, Mark. You're a pal.' She put the phone down. 'Moonchaser,' she said out loud to herself. 'It sounds magical.'

*

Indigo found the rent book without much trouble. It said '1st September - standing order - paid with thanks.' It was signed E.R. Pettigrew. That meant it was paid up until the first of October because rent was nearly always paid in advance. While she was looking for the rent book, she came across a small photo of her dad. He hadn't changed much. There were lines around the eyes and the hairline was a little further back but he still looked very much the way she remembered him.

She slipped the photo into her wallet and went up to see the landlady. Mrs Pettigrew said she was happy for Indigo to stay on until the end of the month. 'I understand, love,' she said kindly and told her to keep the key until October the first.

Back in the flat, Indigo turned on the music centre and began to sift through Paul's CD stack. There were a lot of Buddy Holly collections but she selected an Abba CD, inserted it and pressed play. She sat on the couch for a few minutes and then began to tidy up and arrange things to her taste, to the sound of 'Fernando.' This was going to be her home for the near future. It was her last chance to try to feel closer to her father who had been absent for most of her life.

'Right,' she said, picking up her mobile phone. 'Be brave.'

The phone gave two rings before Clodagh answered it. Clodagh's voice was a bit huffy.

'Indi. How are you?'

'I'm fine Clodagh. I'm at my dad's old flat. I've arranged with the landlady to stay on for a few weeks.' There was no response. 'The rent is paid in advance so it means I don't have to stay in a hotel anymore.'

'Nice of you to let me know.' Clodagh regretted saying it as soon as she had uttered the words. 'I'm sorry,' she went on. 'I know you've got a lot on your plate right now. It's just that I was wondering what had happened to you.'

'I need time Clodagh.'

Silence.

'It's not fair of me to expect you to hang around waiting for me.'

'Right.'

'Don't put your life on hold for me.'

'Are we over then? Is this it?'

'I'm sorry, Clodagh.'

'Me too.' Clodagh's voice was hard now. 'I'm hanging up now. Okay?' Clodagh waited for the words, 'No! Wait!' but they never came.

'Goodbye Clodagh,' said Indigo firmly and she rang off.

Indigo felt nothing but relief. She took a taxi back to her hotel, collected her things and checked out. Another taxi ride later and she was back in the flat. She realised she hadn't eaten for a while. She was quite hungry. There was a small Spar store just up the road. She did a reasonable sized grocery shop, came back and cooked herself some tagliatelle with a carbonara sauce which she had bought in a tub from the shop. She grated some parmesan over it with a good few turns of the pepper mill for seasoning.

She found fresh bedding in the little airing cupboard, made up her bed, then went back into the lounge and watched television until her eyes began to close.

The next day, Thursday, was warm but overcast. The first thing Indigo did after breakfast was to phone Brian Heneghan in the book shop and tell him she wouldn't be back for a while. He was completely understanding and told her not to worry about anything.

She walked to Denmark Street and selected a small shop at random. Joe looked up expectantly when she entered the shop. She was the only customer. Musicians were not known for their early starts.

Indigo said she was looking for a particular guitar and described Paul's guitar as best she could. Joe said 'I've seen a guitar like that, yesterday!'

Indigo's heart began to beat a little faster. 'You didn't sell it, did you?' she asked anxiously.

'No. it belonged to someone. Mark was setting it up.'

'Mark?'

'I'll get him.'

Indigo was left in the silent shop as the young lad went into the back. He returned and told her, 'He's just coming.'

Mark emerged a few moments later He was a slightly built man with a beard, wearing brown cords and a lilac shirt. 'You're asking about the Moonchaser?' he enquired, smiling.

'Moonchaser? Well I'm looking for a guitar with white half moons on the fingerboard.'

'I was working on that very guitar yesterday. It's called an Avocet Moonchaser. From America.'

'Is it for sale?' Indigo was hopeful now.

'No it belongs to someone. The girl who plays in a band called Candyhorse. I was just doing some repairs on it. They gig on Saturday nights in The Singing Kettle. Are you looking to buy it?'

'Yes,' Indigo said. 'Where is the Singing Kettle?'

'Where are you going from?'

'I'm staying at the north end of Great Titchfield Street.'

'It's easy to get to from there. Just hop on the tube at Warren Street Station on the Northern Line. Four stops will take you to Camden Town where the pub is.'

'Thanks so much,' said Indigo turning to leave.

'It's a gorgeous guitar,' said Mark. 'I sometimes go to see Candyhorse so I might see you there.'

Indigo smiled and left the shop. 'Yesssssssssss!' she exclaimed as she stepped outside. Things were looking up.

*

The pub was crowded when Indigo arrived on Saturday night. It had a wooden floor and wooden bar. The bar was shaped like a horseshoe in the centre of the room. Opposite the bar, at either side of the front door as you went in were two raised areas accessed by steps. They were segregated off with handrails and staircase spindles. The one on the left, as you walked in had a blue pool table on it with a light above. The other raised area contained a drum kit, amplifiers and mike stands. There were fancy lights trained on the drum kit. The skin on the front of the bass drum had 'Candyhorse' printed on it.

Behind the bar section was a conservatory where people could eat, and behind that was a tiny beer garden. The pub had a very warm atmosphere. The wood was an antique pine colour. Hanging above the bar area were many black cast iron kettles.

Indigo bought a beer and found a seat very near the stage. She looked around but couldn't guess who the members of the band were. Only a few minutes after she had sat down, two men and two women took to the stage. The blonde girl singer had an absolutely stunning looking guitar. It was white and wide in the body. It had two f shaped holes either side of the strings and all the hardware on it was gold. It looked fantastic. There was no doubt this was the owner of the Moonchaser. Mark had said he had been repairing the Moonchaser so maybe that was why she wasn't using it now.

She loved the band. They sounded a bit like *Prefab Sprout*. Their sound was very sparkly and tight. The songs were a mixture of fast and slow ones. Candyhorse went down very well with the crowd. At the end of each number there were many whistles and hoots of appreciation. Indigo was mesmerised by the singer. The thought that she might have her dad's guitar was very exciting, although how she might have come across it was a question that would need to be answered.

The band got a massive cheer when they were finished. Then all four of them headed for the bar and stood talking amongst themselves. Indigo didn't feel at all shy as she made a beeline for the girl singer. She felt full of confidence and as if luck was on her side.

'Great gig,' she said.

'Thanks,' said Sarah politely, turning to face her.

'I love your guitar. I've never seen anything like it. What's it called?'

'It's a Gretsch White Falcon.' Sarah took her drink from the bar and sipped it slowly.

'Do you collect unusual guitars?'

'No, I've had the Gretsch for a few years now. I've only got one other guitar and that's a Tanglewood acoustic. Do you play yourself?'

Indigo was a bit thrown by the question. 'Um, no but I'm very interested in guitars.'

'You should talk to Frankie, our rhythm guitarist. She has a few nice ones. She just got a rare American one called a Moonchaser. She always plays the Aria in the gigs though. It suits our sound. I'm glad you enjoyed the show.' Sarah smiled and turned to talk to Richard.

Indigo shifted her gaze to fall upon Frankie. She had been so intent on looking at the white guitar that she had barely noticed the other guitar player who had been singing all the harmonies. Frankie was small and slim and very good looking. Her hair was tousled and she was wearing a black T shirt with 'Pocket Rocket' written across it and black jeans.

Just as Indigo was about to make her move, she heard Frankie say loudly, 'Gotta fly guys. See you Tuesday.' And before Indigo could think of something to say, Frankie had left the pub.

'Are you playing here next Saturday?' Indigo asked Sarah, her eyes still on the door.

'Yeah. And we have a gig on Tuesday. Rich; do you have a flyer for Tuesday?' The bass player reached into his back pocket and passed across a small leaflet.

Tuesday 11th September

The Royal Swan

Presents

Candyhorse

With Special Guest

Poet ~ Suzie Rootz

Doors Open at 8pm

Late Licence

'I'll be there,' smiled Indigo. She couldn't wait!

CHAPTER 4

Derek arrived at Frankie's flat at nine in the morning. He had come in his car. She was eating a bacon sandwich and watching the news. He was in a cheerful mood and grabbed her round the waist, kissing her several times. 'Morning beautiful,' he said. 'We're going to see our potential new house today! Are you excited?'

The truth was that she wasn't one bit excited. She would have liked to spend her Sunday morning strumming the Moonchaser and doing a bit of song writing. Since she had found out how much her new guitar was worth, she had decided not to gig it. But she could still write beautiful music on it. She kind of had a song in her head now as a matter of fact, so it was only politeness that made her smile at Derek and say 'Of course I'm excited.'

She loved her flat which she had made very much her own. She wasn't sure how it would be, living with someone. Derek was an enthusiastic kind of guy and always wanted her attention. She wished he wasn't in such a blooming hurry. Or was it Bridie who was in a hurry? God, the idea of living in the same road as Bridie and Patrick made her shudder. Bridie would be popping in every five minutes, running her finger over the furniture to check for dust and generally interfering. She'd have been more excited if she and Derek were getting a little flat of their own somewhere round here. She liked living in Camden.

On the way to the house viewing, Derek sang along to his CDs on his car stereo. He liked eighties music. He was one of those people who always knew all the words to songs and he was singing along now to ABC's 'The look of love.' He was tapping the top of the steering wheel as he drove.

There was a surprise waiting when they pulled up into the drive of the house they were going to view. Bridie and Patrick stood by the front porch. They were smartly dressed and Patrick clutched an A4 pad and pencil in his hand. Bridie waved as she saw them arrive.

'Oh Christ, Derek, what are *they* doing here?' Frankie was very annoyed.

'I didn't know they were going to be here, Frankie. They probably just want to give us their advice. We could do worse than listen to them. My dad knows a lot about houses and they've lived in quite a few.'

'Derek. I'm twenty-three years old. I can make up my mind whether I want to live somewhere without your bloody parents helping me decide.'

'They won't be helping us decide. They're just here to offer advice if we need it.'

'I thought you didn't know they were going to be here.'

'I didn't!'

'Hello, you two!' Bridie was at the passenger window now. 'You might need a cardie, Francine. It's not warm out here.'

'I'm fine,' Frankie replied through gritted teeth and they got out of the car and walked to the front door.

'Now, the first thing you'll want to do is replace this front door,' Patrick began, making a note on his pad. 'It's not very secure and the frame isn't strong.'

Frankie wished herself a million miles away.

It was an Edwardian three bedroom semi. Bridie and Patrick lived in the upper part of the road in a larger double fronted Victorian house. This house that they were viewing today was way out of reach for first time buyers like Frankie and Derek. 'Who is coming up with the money for this?' thought Frankie. But she already knew the answer. 'We'll be beholden to them for years,' she thought.

'Come here you two and look at this.' Patrick was backing into the front garden and craning his neck up to look at the roof. 'Most Edwardian houses have bad roofs,' he explained, with a hand on each shoulder. 'Do you see that sag in the roof? The timbers probably need replacing. It's normal for houses from this era.'

'And I bet you know just the builder to do that work,' Frankie thought. But she said nothing.

The house was long and narrow from front to back. The hallway was long and a corridor stretched to the back of the house. There were two doors to the left and these led to two reception rooms that had been knocked into one. The living room was wider than the dining room because of the way the corridor came round the staircase. There were original sash windows throughout and a small set of French windows at the back of the dining room leading directly into the garden.

Carrying on along the corridor, you stepped down into the kitchen at the back of the house. It needed modernising as it was stuck in the seventies. It had started life as a decent size but someone had portioned off the back of the kitchen and made a shower room and toilet. This prevented a view of the back garden. There was just a narrow passage to the back door.

'Now this is great altogether,' said Bridie enthusiastically. 'If you've got a houseful of kids you don't want them all traipsing through the house to use the upstairs toilet when they're playing outside.'

'You can't go wrong with a downstairs toilet,' agreed Patrick.

'I think it ruins the whole aspect,' announced Frankie. Derek frowned at her.

There was a small forty foot garden with a tiny lawn, patio and small shed at the end. It was a bit overgrown. The fence needed repairing. But the really lovely thing was that there was a beautiful hazelnut tree in the middle of the lawn.

'You can soon cut that thing down,' said Bridie brutally, indicating the tree. 'Trees and lawns don't mix. You'd have your back broken manoeuvring round that with the lawn mower.'

The house had belonged to an old couple. The last of them had died now and it was lying empty. The whole house was in need of a massive amount of repair work and modernisation. It would cost a fortune. Bridie and Patrick were going to enormous lengths to have them in the same road. Derek kept taking Frankie's hand as they went from room to room. She felt suffocated. It was annoying her.

The staircase was very long. At the top was a small back bedroom over the kitchen. There was another corridor upstairs so that you were looking over the staircase all the time. The bathroom and toilet were small. The master bedroom at the front was large.

It had double bay windows. The second bedroom at the side was a small double room.

Every bedroom had a black cast iron small fireplace in it. There was an open fire downstairs. Cracks in the walls had Patrick worrying and making notes.

Is it structurally sound? He wrote. *Does it need under-pinning? Survey?*

Frankie didn't like the house. That windowless dark corridor was very gloomy. The whole place just didn't have a good feel to her.

'We'll need to give it a lot of thought,' she told her future in-laws, tactfully.

'Don't be thinking for too long, now!' This from Patrick as he gave her a patronising nudge with his elbow. 'A little beauty like this house will be snapped up in no time.'

As Derek drove Frankie the short distance to his parent's house she said, 'do you really want to stay in Cricklewood all your life?'

'What's wrong with Cricklewood?'

'Nothing, Derek. It's just that I love living within walking distance of the West End. It's exciting.'

'You won't feel like that when we have a family. Do you want to bring our children up in smoky old central London? Think of the pollution. I'm not having my children growing up in an inner city. It's not safe and it's not healthy.'

'Oh God!' Frankie clenched her fists in frustration. 'I don't want to start a family yet, Derek. We're too young. I want us to have some fun first.'

'You'll change your mind when you've got your own home, nice neighbours and a sweet little garden like that. That property is just crying out for children to bring it to life.'

'Derek, you're rushing me! You all are. You and your parents. I feel like they've rented my womb out just so they can have grandkids - *your* kids – on their doorstep.'

'Don't be obscene.' Derek was getting angry now but they were at the house so he painted on his happy face. Various young Doyle children emerged and stared at Frankie in that way which always disturbed her.

'It's a shame you can't come to Mass with us yet,' said Bridie. 'It'll not be long now until you've had your Instruction and we'll all be going together.'

Frankie forced a weak smile.

It was a nice day for early September. Frankie and Derek sat in the large garden together, sipping a Coke each. Sinead and Siobhan toiled over the roast beef Sunday lunch.

During the meal, with all the children present, Patrick said, 'I've been working on some figures. To make that house habitable will cost around ten thousand.' He smiled over at Bridie. 'I'll get the work done at cost - one of the perks of having family in the trade!'

'You can pay us back at three hundred a month,' beamed Bridie, proudly. When you start at the department store, Francine, you'll be earning a lot more than at that record shop. Uncle Joseph at the bank will be happy to sort you out with a Mortgage.'

'I don't work in a record shop. I sell instruments,' said Frankie sullenly.

'Whatever. You'll probably make a great friend of Deirdre Maloney who works there. She's Colm and Assumpta Maloney's girl. Lovely family! Deirdre is about your age.'

'Well!' said Frankie emphatically as Derek began to drive her home. 'That's our whole life planned out for us. Or should I say *my* whole life! They've picked a house, a builder, my job, my bank manager, my friends - not to mention my religion and taking over my whole damned wedding!'

'*Our* wedding.'

'*Their* wedding, you mean! Don't you think a bride might like to choose her own bloody bridesmaids and colour scheme?'

'I don't know what's wrong with you today, Frankie. They've been nothing but kind to us. Most couples would give anything to have the help they're offering. You're not one bit grateful. I feel slightly disgusted at you from the way you are reacting.'

'And I feel disgusted at your lack of backbone. Don't you want to be captain of your own ship?'

'You talk such rubbish sometimes, Frankie.'

They were silent all the way home after that.

It was a huge relief to get back into her cosy little flat and to be by herself. She cradled the Moonchaser as she sipped from a cold bottle of beer.

*

Indigo checked her reflection in the mirror. She thought she looked not too bad. She was wearing a blue and pink checked shirt and Chinos. She got to the Royal Swan in good time. The gig was excellent. This time, Indigo didn't concentrate so much on the singer and her flashy white guitar. Instead, she directed her eyes to the side of the stage where Frankie was playing a dark red guitar and singing some great harmonies. She was kind of sexy in an understated way.

After their session, Indigo waited fifteen minutes before she approached Frankie at the bar. Frankie was laughing with the barmaid about something. She was still smiling as she turned to face Indigo.

'I loved the gig,' said Indigo, feeling suddenly shy. 'You were really good.'

'Thanks,' said Frankie. She was used to people coming up to them, commenting on the set. 'I saw you on Saturday at the Singing Kettle too.'

'Oh yes. That was my first Candyhorse gig. I actually went there looking for you.'

'You did?' Frankie was surprised and waited to see what the woman was going to say.

'I'm Indigo, by the way.' She stuck out her hand.

'Frankie.' They shook hands briefly.

Now that she was here, Indigo wasn't sure what to say. Frankie waited, still smiling and looking expectant. Finally Indigo said 'It's about your guitar.'

'The Aria? It's a Pro 2 RS 600 Rev Sound. I've had it for many years. Are you looking to buy it? I'm sorry but I'd never sell it. It fits me like a glove.'

'Yes, I could see that when I watched you playing. Can we sit down?'

'Sure. Are you from Ireland? My fiancé is Irish. Well, his parents are. What part are you from?'

'The west,' said Indigo as they took their seats. They sat away from the stage where the poet was chanting a rhyme.

'Oh. Derek's parents are from Leitrim and Clare, I think. I've never been to Ireland.'

'Haven't you? I'd never been to England until this trip.'

'Welcome to London. How long are you staying?'

'Until the end of the month, probably. I'm staying in a friend's flat.'

'Do you like it so far?'

'I do,' said Indigo enthusiastically. 'I like the buzz of the city.'

'So you're a guitarist?' asked Frankie. 'Do you play in a band?'

'No, I don't play. I wish I did.'

'I give guitar lessons,' grinned Frankie and flipped a business card out of her wallet and handed it to Indigo.

Frankie Green

Guitar Lessons

Acoustic or Electric

Beginners to Advanced

There was a phone number at the bottom.

'I'd love to learn one day. Is it hard work, teaching I mean?'

'It's fun, mostly. You get all sorts. The difficult ones are usually the guys who want to be able to play "Sultans of Swing" after two lessons.' They both laughed. 'So why are you interested in my Aria, Indigo?' Frankie looked directly into her eyes. Indigo shifted under her gaze. Frankie was very attractive and had a really nice speaking voice. It was slightly posh and a little husky.

'I'm actually interested in your Moonchaser.'

Frankie's eyebrows shot up. 'How did you know about that?

'I was speaking to Mark, the guy who fixes guitars in Denmark Street. I went into that shop looking for a Moonchaser and he told me he'd just fixed one up for you.'

'So much for customer confidentiality,' Frankie breathed, ironically.

'I came to the gig so I could see it. But you left the Singing Kettle before I had a chance to ask you about it.'

'So here you are!'

'Here I am!' They both smiled now.

'Well Indigo. I've only had the Moonchaser for a week, but I already know I don't want to sell it. You see, I'm in love.'

Indigo looked totally confused. 'You mean your fiancé?'

'No I mean the guitar, silly! Well, him too, obviously. I don't know where you'd find another Moonchaser. According to Mark there were only a handful made in 1969 in America. So you might want to start searching there. It's a long way to go for a

46

guitar. Where did you see one when you first decided you wanted one?'

Indigo didn't want to say too much. 'My dad had one. When I was little.'

'Ah I see. What happened to it?'

'I don't know,' said Indigo vaguely.

'My dad played guitar too. That's how I got interested. He passed away when I was seventeen.'

'Oh, I'm sorry,' said Indigo, quickly.

'He used to sit on the end of my bed,' Frankie continued. 'When I was a young kid. He'd strum his guitar and sing me to sleep. I loved it.'

Indigo was hanging onto Frankie's every word and looking at her with what looked like tears in her eyes. Frankie noticed. 'What did he play?' Indigo asked softly.

'My favourite one was a country and western one. It went, "Close your sleepy eyes, my little buckaroo." I kind of thought the song was all about me at that age.' Frankie laughed but Indigo didn't.

'You must miss him,' said Indigo seriously.

'I wanted to be just like him,' said Frankie, leaning back.' That's why I took up the guitar.'

'What kind of guitar did he have?'

'An Eko acoustic with an elaborate stainless steel pick up attachment that he wedged into the sound hole. I have the Eko guitar now.'

'How lovely,' replied Indigo. 'I bet you look after it really carefully.'

'I do, but it's almost impossible to play. The action is too high. It means it's really hard to hold down a chord. It kills your fingers. How he struggled on with it for all those years is a mystery.'

'You can play that song to your own little buckaroos one day, on their grandfather's guitar.'

'Oh God, not you as well!'

'What did I say?'

Frankie laughed. 'Nothing. It's just that everyone seems to be wanting to get me pregnant lately.'

'I don't want to get you pregnant!' said Indigo, suppressing a smile and with a twinkle in her eye. She saw Frankie blush slightly at the flirty remark.

'What would you play if you learned the guitar?' asked Frankie, changing the subject.

'Buddy Holly,' said Indigo without thinking. 'Everything he ever wrote.'

CHAPTER 5

Indigo sat in the small kitchen in the flat in Great Titchfield Street. She was sitting on a high wooden barstool with both elbows on the worktop. Her mobile phone lay on the counter and in her hands she twirled a small business card over and over. It was Frankie's card, the one she had given Indigo last night.

Finally she picked up the phone and punched in the number.

'Hello. Frankie?'

'Yes?'

'It's Indigo here. From last night.'

'I *thought* I recognized the accent. How are you doing?'

'I'm fine thanks. How are you?'

'Good, thanks. I have a day off today so I'm being ultra lazy. Have you had any luck looking for a Moonchaser?'

'No, but I've been thinking. I'd like to book a couple of guitar lessons.'

'Oh, really?'

'Yes. I'd like to see if I like it before I actually buy a guitar.'

'Do you have a guitar to practise on, Indigo?'

'You can call me Indi - most people do.'

'Okay, Indi.'

'No, I don't have a guitar.'

'Well, I don't know of any Moonchasers for sale, but we do have a fabulous guitar in the shop I work in. It's perfect for a beginner. Actually it's made by a company in Ireland of all places. It's £160 but you get a great guitar for the money. Do you like white guitars? I mean, I'm assuming you want an electric.'

'White? Yeah. Is it like your singer's guitar?'

'Sarah's guitar? No it's nothing at all like that. Sarah's guitar costs a lot more than £160! The one I'm thinking of only comes in white as far as I know. It looks great and is very nice to play.'

'Wouldn't I be better getting something for about £50, until I see if I'm any good?'

'A cheap guitar can really put you off playing if it's difficult to play. It's up to you of course though.'

'I'll go with whatever you recommend.'

'Great, well I'm in work on Monday so you could see it then and we could decide when you want your lessons. The place I work is called Harmonix. On Denmark Street.' Frankie paused and then rushed on. 'Are you doing anything on Sunday Indi?'

'Um, no. Not really.'

'Would you like me to show you round the markets?' Frankie wasn't sure why she had suggested this. But she had really liked Indi on first meeting her. There was a touch of sadness about her but she was funny and vibrant. She thought they could maybe be friends. She heard the smile in her new friend's voice as she replied,

'I'd love to.'

*

On Sunday morning, Frankie was ready in good time. She was just about to leave when she saw Derek pull up outside.

'Oh Shit!' she said. She went down and let him in. He kissed her and then frowned and said, 'You're not wearing that are you? Mum will have a fit! You're supposed to be in a dress.' Frankie was wearing jeans and a colourful stripy jumper.

'Sorry, Derek, I totally forgot about the Communion. I've made other plans.'

'Well you'll have to unmake them, fast! Mum and dad are expecting us.' Derek was looking horrified now.

'I can't unmake them. Sorry. I'm meeting someone'

'Who are you meeting?' He was suddenly suspicious. 'A man?'

'No, a woman. One of my students. She's not from London so I'm showing her around today.'

Derek took a deep breath. 'Let me get this straight.' He held his hands out in front of him. 'You're missing Ronan's Holy Communion to take a student shopping? Have you lost your mind, Frankie?'

Frankie was defiant. 'No, Derek. I think I've found my own mind, actually. I'm not going to the Communion because I'm sick of your family trying to run my life. I need a break from them.'

'Well it's tough that you feel that way because this is the biggest day in Ronan's life and you ARE going. Now stop being silly and go and get changed.' Derek gave her a little push in the small of her back in the direction of her bedroom.

'I've said "no" and I mean "no". Now would you mind going because I'm running late now.'

'You absolute bitch.' Derek's voice was cold now. 'I can't believe you'd let down a child.'

'Oh, Ronan doesn't care if I'm there or not and you know it. It's your parents who want to parade me around like a prize poodle to all their friends. I'm not going. Now would you please leave?'

'You haven't heard the last of this, Frankie.' Derek's face had gone white with anger. 'Not by a long shot.' He stormed out and Frankie let out a sigh of relief. Her hands were shaking slightly. A few moments later she heard his wheels spin on the road outside as he sped away.

*

Frankie had regained her composure by the time she met Indigo at the entrance to Camden tube station. When she arrived Indigo was standing there with a huge smile on her face.

'Sorry I'm a bit late, Indi,' said Frankie a little breathlessly. 'I got delayed'

'No problem at all.' The two women began to walk in the direction of the markets.

'I could do with a coffee first, if you don't mind,' said Frankie.

'Great idea. How about this place?' Indigo had spotted an organic café on the canal banks. They went in and found a seat. They ordered two coffees and each had a slice of cake. 'I'm always hungry in the mornings,' grinned Indigo.

'I had a bit of a row with my boyfriend this morning,' said Frankie suddenly. 'Well he's my fiancé actually.' Indigo immediately looked at Frankie's left hand and for the first time, noticed the diamond ring there.

'Oh? Not too serious I hope.'

'The row or my relationship with him?'

Indigo looked puzzled then grasped Frankie's meaning and smiled. 'The row,' she said.

Frankie sipped her coffee. 'Well, it was quite serious. I'm supposed to be at his little brother's Holy Communion today.

'Oh no! You didn't miss that to take me round the markets did you? I mean, I can go anytime.' Indi looked worried.

'No, no. It's a long story. His parents are very, very overbearing. It's just all got too much for me this week.'

'Holy Communion is a BIG deal back in Ireland. They make a huge fuss,' said Indigo emphatically.

'I think this event is to be a huge thing too. I mean, they've hired a marquee, for God's sake.'

'You'll be right out of favour with them now then,' said Indigo.

'They've just been slowly suffocating me over the past few months. They've planned my whole wedding, chosen my bridesmaids and the dresses and the church.' Frankie ticked off each annoying thing on her fingers with her other hand. 'They've chosen us a house – in the same road as them; decided where we're getting our mortgage; picked me out a new job; decided who I should be friends with...' She tailed off, shaking her head.

'They sound like a nightmare.' agreed Indigo. 'Is he a bit of a mummy's boy?' She finished her cake and licked her fingers.

'He's under the thumb of both of them,' said Frankie. 'He works for his dad and still lives at home.

They say "jump" and he says "how high?"' She suddenly asked, 'Do you have a boyfriend?'

'Nah. I had a girlfriend until a week or so ago.'

Frankie's cheeks flushed and she was completely stumped for words. Then she said in a small voice, 'oh,' and then they both giggled, shyly.

'Is is hard being gay in the West of Ireland?'

'I haven't had any hassle. The only one who's never accepted it is my mum.'

'How old were you when you came out to her?'

'Fourteen.'

'Really?' Frankie was astonished.

'Yeah, I was a fan of this boy band and one day one of them came out as gay. So my mum was saying, "I'd have never have guessed that about him." We were actually sitting at the tea table and I just said, "I'm like him, Mum. I'm gay too."'

'What did she say?'

'She kept saying "what rubbish!" but deep down, I think she knew it was true. She's never liked me very much.'

'That's a strange thing to say about your mother.'

'We've never been close.' Indigo changed the subject. 'What does he look like- your fiancé?'

'Well, you've seen him, actually.'

'I have?' Indigo looked surprised.

'Yeah, he's the drummer for Candyhorse.'

'Oh *him*! He's hunky isn't he?'

Frankie leaned in a little closer. 'Have you ever fancied a man, Indi?'

Indi grinned. 'No, just thousands of women. But I can appreciate a man for his good looks.'

'Thousands?' said Frankie; and they both laughed again.

*

Camden markets turned out to be the most colourful place Indigo had ever been. There were decorated buildings everywhere. There was life on every corner. The streets thronged with people. There were bars, cafes, tattoo parlours and body piercing places. Everywhere you looked there were clothes decorating the front of the shops, advertising what was inside. There were theatrical costumes, gothic outfits and every trendy rig out you could imagine.

African and Native American jewellery adorned stall fronts along with wind chimes, arts crafts and pottery. There were dozens of shoe shops and hat shops and places where you could exchange records and CDs.

Indigo bought a white cowboy hat and put it on. It really suited her. They browsed for ages in a shop selling rare DVDs.

A man went past on a scooter with a clip board attached to his handlebars. 'What is he doing?' asked Indigo, sounding puzzled.

'He's doing The Knowledge,' replied Frankie. 'That's how taxi drivers practice.'

'What; you mean he picks people up and gives them lifts on the back to places?'

Frankie laughed. 'No. They get to know where all the little streets are that way. It's easier to get about on a scooter.' She paused and went on. 'Do you like scooters and motorbikes?'

'I do, yeah.'

'Is it too early for a drink?'

'It's never too early for a drink!'

'I know just the place.'

The bar was facing the canal. To Indigo's delight, instead of bar stools there was a line of Vespa scooters for patrons to sit on. Only the back end of each scooter was there. The people looked so funny all sitting astride the bikes, having drinks. She absolutely loved it and they took their seats and ordered bottled beer.

'I'd have taken you to the Portobello Road markets as well but they are closed on a Sunday,' said Frankie as they sipped beer. 'The Stables market is just on the other side. There are a lot of antiques there.'

'What is this canal called?'

'This is the Regent's Canal. It's one of the arms of the Grand Union Canal and is an actual lock. This is the Paddington arm. The Grand Union Canal comes down from Birmingham. The main waterway comes out at Brentford onto the River Thames. That's the Putney area. It turns left at Uxbridge onto Regent's Canal and goes through the centre of London - Little Venice, Camden – through the city to Limehouse Basin. It would have been a major trade route transporting goods from Birmingham to the docks in London at one time.'

Indigo was gazing intently at Frankie as she talked. 'You are so knowledgeable,' she said.

'Well, I've lived here all my life. I do love London. It's so... alive!'

'It's so different where I live.'

56

'I bet it's beautiful though. You've got such a small population in Ireland compared to us. It must be good to just have all that lovely scenery to yourself.'

'Maybe you'll come over and visit me there one day,' said Indigo.

'Do you live by yourself? I picture you in a little thatched cottage with lots of cats and a donkey in the garden.'

Indigo laughed. 'No cats or donkeys, sorry! But I do share a house with someone. She's called Gillian. Oh, and we have a normal roof. But it is kind of out in the sticks. We have sheep and cows wandering up the road.'

'Is Gillian your ex-girlfriend?'

'No. She's just a friend. Straight. Have you ever dated a woman?'

'No. Why do you ask that?' said Frankie.

'Oh, I just got a sort of gay vibe off you when I first saw you.'

'Ooh! I never knew I was giving off those kinds of vibes! Shall we have another beer?'

'Great idea!'

They talked long into the afternoon and when they left they were more than slightly tipsy.

'Do you want to go back to my flat and see the Moonchaser?' asked Frankie. 'It's just a short walk away.'

'Oh yes, I'd really like to see it. And where you live.'

They walked to the end of the markets, past a small park and some tennis courts until they came to Frankie's flat. As soon as they entered the living room, Indigo saw the guitar, perched on a stand in the corner. The afternoon sunshine was coming through the window, bathing the white moon inlays in light.

'Wow,' said Indigo, reverently. She walked over to it and touched the strings softly. 'It's so long since I've seen a guitar like this.' She said 'It's so beautiful. Will you play it for me?'

'Sure. What would you like to hear?' Frankie came over and carefully picked the Moonchaser up. She sat on the couch and plugged a lead into a large amp which was nearby. She ran through some notes and chords for a few seconds, and then looked at Indigo expectantly.

'Play anything. Whatever's your favourite.'

'Okay.' Frankie began to play and then started to sing. It was *Rocket Man*, the Elton John song. Indigo knew this one and joined in with the singing. The guitar sounded wonderful. They got to the end of the song.

Indigo said, 'You play and sing so well. The guitar has a great sound.'

'Thanks. Does your dad still play?'

Indigo walked over to the window. She stared out for the longest time. Frankie sensed something was wrong and waited. Finally Indigo said, 'He died. Two and a half weeks ago.'

'Oh, Indi. I'm so sorry.' Frankie put the guitar on the sofa, went over and put her arms round Indigo's neck, very gently. It was the first human contact Indigo had experienced since she had been in London and she had to fight the urge to grab Frankie and hold her tightly. They stood like that for some moments.

'Would another beer be a good idea?' Frankie finally said. 'I have some cold bottles in the fridge.'

Indigo nodded. They sat together on the couch with the beers.

'So that's why you're in London?'

'Yes. The funeral was on the fourth of September. He died on the first. I wasn't there when he did. I didn't know. A friend of my dad's let my mum know, but she didn't want to go to the funeral.'

'You went by yourself?'

'Yes. I'm staying in his old flat. In Great Titchfield Street. Sorting out his stuff and that.'

'How long was it since you saw him?' Frankie's voice was soft and kind.

'Twenty years. He left when I was seven.'

'You had no contact in all that time?'

'No, I just knew he'd gone to London.'

'So finding a Moonchaser is important because it reminds you so much of him?'

Indigo didn't want to explain the whole truth at this time. She was desperate to ask where Frankie had got the guitar but scared of the answer she might get.

'Yeah. I've been feeling a bit emotional about it since he died.'

'It's almost like we were meant to meet,' said Frankie, because I only got the Moonchaser a little while ago, from a pawn shop not far from here. That's a huge coincidence, that you were nearby and looking for one the same. Especially as there were only a handful of them made.'

Indigo felt so relieved that Frankie had come across the guitar honestly. She would have been devastated if Frankie had been the thief. She had never really thought for one minute she could have been, but it was good to have it confirmed. Whoever took the guitar obviously sold it straight away to the pawn shop. She had no doubt that the instrument she had just been listening to was her dad's old guitar. He had left it to Indigo and by rights she should have it. But she was happy just to stay close to it and the young woman who now possessed it.

'I still want to take lessons,' said Indigo. 'I want to learn; even if I don't find my own Moonchaser.'

'We can sort the lessons out tomorrow. I can probably fit you in for a half hour lesson tomorrow as well,' Frankie replied. After a pause, she went on. 'What happened to your dad?'

'He had cancer. He was only forty-seven.'

'That's so sad. You know you said you wanted to learn Buddy Holly songs? Was that what he used to play? When you were little I mean?'

'Yes, all the time. He used to sit on the end of my bed when I was a kid and play.'

'Just like my dad,' said Frankie. 'We have so much in common.'

'We do,' agreed Indigo. 'What was your dad like?'

'He was small and kind of strong looking. He had been an amateur boxer in his youth. He had black hair and the kind of heavy beard growth that needs to be shaved twice a day. He was very quiet and sort of shy, for a man. He loved country and western music, especially Charlie Pride and Johnny Cash. He was always playing his guitar. When I think of him, I always think of him playing and singing.'

I found a photo of my dad in his flat,' said Indigo, taking out her wallet. 'I think it was quite recent, because he looks in his mid forties in it.' Indigo took out the photo and handed it to Frankie.

'That's Paul Keane!' Frankie sounded shocked. 'Paul Keane was your dad?'

'You knew my dad?'

'I didn't know he had died, but yes, I knew Paul. He used to come to the Candyhorse gigs.'

Indigo just stared at Frankie, trying to take this in.

'He used to come every Saturday, to the Singing Kettle.'

The two women stared at one another for a few seconds then Frankie looked back at the photograph then up at Indigo.

'He used to come to the gigs with his boyfriend.'

'His boyfriend?'

'Yes. Carl.'

CHAPTER 6

Indigo lay in bed in her flat. It was only 5.20am but she was wide awake. At length, she got up and made a mug of tea and brought it back to bed.

Her dad had been gay. Just like her. It was something that had never occurred to her but a few things now fell into place. She didn't have to look at the letter her dad had dictated when he was dying to remember the words he had used. She knew them by heart.

I couldn't stay. It was killing me.

Now those words made sense. He must have meant that living a straight life with her mother was unbearable. Indigo was quite happy to be 'out and proud.' But things must have been different for a gay man in Ireland in 1984, which was the year her parents got married. People were afraid to come out back then. They lived sad lives with partners they did not love and never experienced fully being their true selves. How very sad that was.

London was the place people ran to. London was liberal and up to date. Being gay was no big deal in London.

What had her father's life been like when he arrived in the big city? Was he lonely? Did he find friends quickly? So many questions would never be answered. Of course, Carl must know a lot about her dad. But she already knew that she wasn't going to try to find him. Her dad was entitled to his privacy. Even in death.

Frankie hadn't known much. She just knew Paul and Carl as part of the gang of people who drank in the Singing Kettle and liked to watch Candyhorse. They were known as a gay couple. Yes, she had spoken to Paul, but only small talk.

Her mum must have known. Or suspected. It might explain her general attitude of sullen resentment. It can't have been very nice for a woman to think she was marrying the man of her dreams only to later find out that he might be gay. No wonder her mum was hostile to her when she came out herself. The whole gay topic must be like a thorn under her skin. One that she did not need reminding of seven years after losing her husband.

This wasn't the only subject keeping her awake. She had had the most wonderful day yesterday with Frankie. It was great to have found a new friend. But Indigo now found herself very attracted to Frankie who was not only a straight woman, but a woman betrothed to someone else. Frankie was everything she wanted in a girlfriend. She was good looking, sexy, funny, kind and intelligent. What was the point of spending more time with her? She'd only have her heart broken in the end when Frankie married her drummer man.

Why was she still in London? She had tracked down the guitar. Okay, it wasn't hers as it should have been but it was in very safe and deserving hands. She should go home now. But going home would mean not seeing Frankie again. She would stay until the end of the month. Leaving now just wasn't an option, somehow.

She was looking forward to having a guitar lesson later today. Or to be more truthful she was looking forward to seeing Frankie again. It would be good to see her in her work environment. She had something to attend to first.

Indigo watched television until nine. The programmes were light breakfast shows about fashion, cooking and babies. When it was time, she went upstairs and knocked on Mrs Pettigrew's door.

'Mrs Pettigrew, I'll come straight to the point. A guitar has gone missing from my dad's flat; it was missing on the first day I arrived here. The case is there but no guitar. That guitar was left to me. The only conclusion I can come to is that someone else had a key and took it, between my dad going into hospital and me arriving here. Now are you sure no one else has been in there?' Her tone was firm and commanding.

'Nobody, lovie. Only yourself.'

'Then I'm afraid I'll have to involve the police. I just thought I would tell you because they're bound to want to ask you some questions.' She was bluffing. It worked.

'Now, now there's no need for the police to be called, I'm sure,' said Mrs Pettigrew, nervously. 'I was asked not to tell you this but in the circumstances I suppose you need to know. Your mother was over here, the Saturday before you came. She didn't want you to be upset any more than you were. She thought you might be distressed that she wasn't going to the funeral. I think she had business to sort out.'

So that was it. Her mother!

'Did my mother take anything? It's very important, Mrs Pettigrew.'

'Well I don't think I should have been put in this position between the two of you. What a carry on. But now that it's all out in the open...she had a car with her and made several trips out to it with bags of stuff. I didn't see what. I can't be expected to be in charge of someone's things. She said she was his wife. I don't see...'

'It's alright,' Indigo interrupted. 'I just needed to know a stranger hadn't been here taking his things. Thank you. I'm sorry you were put in an awkward position.' She hurried back down the stairs.

Her mother must have taken anything that was valuable and pawned it. At least she knew now. Her mother had no right to do that. She was not the next of kin. But Indigo did not intend to question her mother about it. It was in her mother's nature to be mercenary. Indigo wanted as little contact as possible with the woman.

She had felt like she had no family for a long time now. Nothing had changed. She was angry with her mother but not exactly surprised. She shut a door in her mind to it and decided to concentrate on the present.

Toady was going to be a good day. She was going to see Frankie. And she was more than a little excited about getting a guitar of her own for the first time in her life, even if it wasn't the Moonchaser.

*

65

There was a nice smell to the shop Frankie worked in. She thought it was furniture polish but she wasn't sure. Frankie greeted her warmly.

'Now. Before we go up for your first lesson, let's see about this guitar.' She led Indigo over to a rack of guitars hanging from the wall and selected a white slim looking electric guitar with gold hardware. Indigo gasped when she saw the fingerboard. It was black and featured, instead of dot markers, an elaborate vine pattern, winding its way up the neck.

'I thought you'd like the fret board design,' grinned Frankie. 'It's called the tree of life.'

'It's beautiful,' Indigo smiled back. 'What's this bit here?' she pointed to a bar attached to bridge.

'That's your tremolo arm. You'll look like a proper little Buddy Holly playing that!'

Indigo bought the guitar gladly and then followed Frankie up the stairs to the next floor where she gave lessons. They took Indigo's new guitar with them and the lesson was given on that. Frankie tuned it first and then put a thick leather strap on it. Indigo put the strap over her head and tried to get comfy.

She was told the names of all the parts of the guitar and the names of the strings. It was a bit confusing when Frankie referred to Indigo's fingers as 'your first finger' or 'your third finger'. Indigo had to keep looking and thinking about which was which.

Playing chords was much harder than she had imagined. 'Oh jeez! How do you manage to change from one to the other so quickly? I'll never be able to do it that quickly!'

'It seems that way at the beginning, but you'll soon master it,' said Frankie, kindly. Frankie kept telling Indigo to relax her left arm and hand and to let her wrist drop when she was playing a chord.

'Like this?' said Indigo, her wrist still very tense. Frankie stood behind her and slipped her left arm under Indigo's.

'See how my wrist is?' she asked, holding down a chord shape. 'Now you try it.' Indigo tried and Frankie gently pulled Indigo's wrist further down.

Frankie was hands-on with all her students. She had stood behind many budding guitarists with her arms under theirs, gently moving their hands into position. But she had never before felt so conscious of the nearness of someone. She could smell Indigo's perfume and noticed the softness of her skin. It felt right to be so close and yet dangerous. Frankie was becoming flustered. She backed off and moved back to her position facing Indigo. They went on with the lesson.

Indigo was trying to concentrate on what they were doing, but she too was acutely aware of the nearness of the other woman. It seemed quite intimate. Indigo loved being close to Frankie. She was really happy to be in her company again.

At the end Frankie said, 'You might want to buy a case for that. You don't want it bashed about.'

'It's okay', said Indigo. 'There is a case back at the flat which I'm sure will fit. What time do you finish here?'

'Three o'clock.'

'Want to do something?'

'Sure. What did you have in mind?'

'Well it's very typically touristy, but I'd love to see Madame Tussauds.'

'What a fabulous idea. It'll be fun.'

'My treat, of course,' said Indigo. 'Right. I'll take the guitar home and meet you back here at three.'

Indigo took a taxi back to the flat because of having the guitar with her. Frankie gave her a shaped box to protect it on the journey. When she got back she found that it fitted her dad's case perfectly. She was aware of feeling elated and knew why. Frankie was all she could think about. Yes, it was official. She had done the very thing lesbians are supposed to avoid. She had fallen for a straight girl.

*

Frankie was working in the music shop for the rest of the day, until three o'clock. She was extremely distracted and dreamy. What was it about Indigo that had her so interested? Was it some kind of curiosity because Indigo was gay? No, it was more than that. She had to admit it. She was attracted to the Irish woman. Her first gay crush. She decided to relax and go with the feeling. It felt absolutely delicious.

*

Indigo and Frankie were enjoying an Italian meal in a trendy little restaurant in Saint Christopher's Place. They had both enjoyed the tour round Madame Tussauds. It had been many years since Frankie was there and it was Indigo's first visit. They had built up quite an appetite so the food was welcome.

'This is very appropriate that we should be eating in Saint Christopher's Place,' said Indigo as she ate.

'Oh, why's that?'

'Well, he was the patron saint of travellers. I'll be travelling back soon. Back to the emerald isle.'

'When do you go back?'

'In less than two weeks time.'

Frankie wasn't sure how to answer. She wanted to say, 'I'll miss you' but it sounded a bit forward. She was saved from having to respond by a vibration in her pocket from her mobile phone. It was on the silent setting but she still knew when a message was coming in. She glanced discreetly at the screen. It was from Derek.

Outside your flat - where are you?

She didn't want to start texting at the table so she ignored it for now but immediately began to worry that Derek would be getting annoyed. Indigo had seen her look at the phone.

'Everything alright?' she asked.

'Yeah it's just Derek, looking for me.'

'How are things between you at the moment?'

'Oh! Don't ask!' Frankie changed the subject. 'When would you like to have your next guitar lesson?'

'How about Thursday?

'Thursday sounds fine. Don't forget to practise!'

'I won't forget. I'd love to be able to play like you.'

Frankie smiled and ran her fingers through her hair.

'How do you get your hair like that?' asked Indigo, admiringly. Frankie was flustered.

'I just wash it and it ends up this way. I suppose it's the cut.'

Indigo almost said that it looked beautiful but began folding her napkin instead.

They got a taxi home. Frankie got out first at her flat.

'Bye,' said Indigo. Impetuously, she added, 'thanks for the date.'

Frankie was embarrassed at the comment but hadn't time to think about it, as Derek's car was waiting outside her flat. She approached the driver's door as the taxi sped away.

'Where have you been?' demanded Derek. I've been sitting here for forty-five minutes.'

'I was at Madame Tussauds and then had a bite to eat.'

'Who was that in the taxi with you?'

'It was a new friend I've got. I met her at one of our gigs.'

'What's her name?'

Frankie was slightly irritated by Derek giving her the third degree but she answered. 'Indigo.'

'Was this the one you missed the Communion for?'

Frankie sighed. 'Yes. Are you coming in?'

When they were inside the flat he said 'She must be pretty special, this Indigo, seeing as you're spending every hour God sends with her.'

'That's a slight exaggeration. She's on holiday and I'm showing her around.'

'How very nice of you.' Derek's voice was dripping with sarcasm. 'Ronan was very upset you weren't at his Holy Communion. And I looked a right idiot with everyone asking where you were.' He began pacing the room. 'You've changed, Frankie. When I first met you, you were always happy and smiling. You always looked pleased to see me. Now you can barely give me the time of day. You don't know how much that hurts.'

'Derek, I've explained that I need a break from the pressure your parents are putting on me... and yes, a break from you.'

'You want a break from me? What sort of break?' He was standing stock still, facing her now.

Frankie decided to grab this opportunity. 'I think it's best if we don't see each other for a while.' She looked him in the eye. He went white and in a flash he had punched the wall, just to the side of her head. Then cradling his injured hand he ran out and down to his car, without saying anything.

Frankie noticed her hands were shaking slightly. She found a bottle of brandy she had in a cupboard, poured two inches and knocked it straight back. Then she went into the bedroom, pulled the curtains and got into bed.

*

The house was a very ordinary semi, with peeling paint and net curtains in the windows. Indigo didn't know what she had been expecting. Possibly something more dramatic. When she rang the bell, a blonde woman emerged from the back doorway and called her over. 'You can come this way,' she said. 'Keith is ready for you. Just go straight in; through there.' The woman pointed to a door off the kitchen and Indigo gingerly opened it and went into the room.

She had never been to a psychic medium before and she was quite nervous. The man was sitting in semi-darkness which scared her. It seemed spooky. He had the curtains closed. The only light in the room was from a dim lamp.

'Hello,' he said, remaining seated in an armchair. 'You must be Indigo.'

'Yes. Hello.'

He gestured towards the couch and she perched on the edge of the cushion. He had black wavy hair and a very thick, dark moustache. He was wearing jeans and a light grey sweatshirt.

'Now, the first thing I need to do is to get a piece of jewellery from you. I get vibrations from items like that, you see. Have you got something you've worn for a long time?'

Indigo's hand went straight to her necklace. 'My cross,' she said, undoing the clasp. It was a simple Celtic cross with a small jewel in the centre. The cross was suspended from a black lace. She passed it over to Keith. She was very apprehensive now.

In the corner on a small table, a telephone started to ring. It sounded very loud in the atmosphere of the darkened room. 'Oh, I'm sorry,' said Keith. 'I forgot to disconnect it. It won't happen again.' He leaned over the arm of his chair and pulled the telephone jack from its socket in the wall. The telephone was silenced, mid-ring.

He curled Indigo's necklace in the palm of one hand and seemed to press down hard on it with his other hand. His eyes were closed and his breathing was slightly audible now that the room was silent again.

'I have a male presence here. He's not young but not old either. I'm feeling that this man is your father.'

Indigo forgot to be scared. She leaned forward, her hands clutching her knees.

'I feel that he passed quite recently. He's conveying to me that he loves you very much and he's sorry. Sorry he wasn't there enough. He's very content in the spirit world. I can see him smiling and he's saying he's with Jack.'

'That's my Grandpa.' Tears came into her eyes but she fought to control herself.

'Yes, he's with Jack and they're both proud of you,' Keith went on, his eyes still closed. Suddenly he opened his eyes and looked at Indigo. 'Have you been looking for something recently? Something that was lost or went missing?' His eyes closed again.

'Yes,' said Indigo in a very small voice.

'He's grateful to you. He's happy that you found it.'

Indigo relaxed as Keith went on with the reading.

*

Frankie dreamed that she was in a boat. It was a small wooden rowing boat and she was being rowed across a lake. There were smoky blue mountains up ahead, and in the distance, a small sandy shore. Just visible, beyond the water's edge was a tiny cottage with smoke coming out of the chimney.

She looked back to see where she had come from and saw that another boat was on the water. Paul Keane was pulling on the oars and Indigo sat, very still in the other boat. She didn't look at Frankie. Her gaze was fixed on the shore.

Overhead, a large heron flew above the two boats, his wing beats very slow and ponderous.

They seemed to be on the lake for a long time. Frankie could see the water; inky blue but with a thick film on the top, like dust.

Indigo's boat began to catch up with hers and then it glided by. Indigo still did not seem to see her. It neared the shore and Paul jumped out and pulled it up onto the sand. Indigo climbed out of the boat and without looking back, walked into the cottage.

Then her own boat was being pulled up onto the sand and she climbed out too. She walked to the cottage and knocked on the door. As the door was opened from the inside, Frankie glanced back across the lake and saw the two boats pulling away again, side by side. Paul did not look at her but the other boatman smiled and waved as he rowed away. It was her own dad, Jack.

CHAPTER 7

Blake was a fast learner and soon picked up the drum patterns for Candyhorse's songs. Richard, Sarah and Frankie were impressed. Blake was being well paid to stand in for Derek and he had always been a bit of a fan of the band. So he was happy to be here, at the rehearsal. He was a very easy going man and they all got on well with him.

Derek had phoned Sarah to say he had hurt his hand changing a tyre on his car and wouldn't be able to play the drums this Saturday. He had not been in touch with Frankie and she was glad about this. Now she might get the space she needed.

She also needed and wanted space from Indigo, despite the fact that their next guitar lesson was tomorrow. She hadn't decided yet whether to cancel it or not. Frankie had been very perturbed since Indi had shouted, 'thanks for the date,' from the back of the taxi on Monday evening. Did Indigo really see Frankie as a potential girlfriend? It would seem so, and the thought was very worrying.

Frankie had never had a lesbian experience and had never developed feelings for another female before. But she knew she did have feelings for Indi already and this startled her.

She was supposed to be marrying Derek. She was soon to become his wife. So why did everything about her relationship with him suddenly feel wrong? She and Derek had had the biggest row they had ever had on Monday night and yet she had only dreamed of Indigo. She seemed to be falling out of love with a man and right into love with a woman. What was wrong with her?

*

Indigo knew this was going to be a difficult phone call, and she was ready.

'Hello Mum?'

'Indigo. Are you back in Ireland?'

'No, I'm still in London.'

'What are you doing still there?'

Indigo decided to cut to the chase. She was almost sure that Frankie's Moonchaser was the one that had been owned by Paul but she had to be certain.

'I know you were over here, Mum. The landlady told me.' There was an audible 'humf,' from her mother before she replied.

'That interfering old cow! She should keep her nose out of other folks' business. I was just seeing to a few things there.'

Indigo was undeterred. 'Did you take Dad's guitar? I'm asking because he left that guitar to me in a letter.'

'What letter?' Her mother was suddenly interested now.

'He left a short letter with his friend, Carl.'

'Oh. Him!'

'Did you pawn it, Mum? I need to know.'

Noleen was not good at keeping up pretences when she was cornered. She caved in easily. 'I took it to a place in Kentish Town. I only got a few pounds for it.'

76

So, Indigo had been right. She didn't bother asking Noleen what else she had taken. She rang off with the shortest of farewells.

*

After the rehearsal, Frankie invited herself back to Richard's house for a drink. She said she wanted to talk to him about a few things.

'I've got some stuff going on at the minute, Richard that might affect the band.'

Richard handed Frankie a beer. 'What stuff?'

Frankie took a deep breath. 'Well you know I'm supposed to be marrying Derek?'

'Yes.'

'Well, I have decided I'm just not ready for marriage and children and all that. I'm only twenty-three, Richard. I want to live a bit first.'

'I see. Does Derek know this yet?'

'He knows we are on a break.'

'How did he take that?'

'Not well. He punched the wall in my flat when I told him. That's how he really hurt his hand.'

'Wow. That must have been scary.'

'It was. I've really had enough of him lately.'

'Hmm. I guess that's going to make playing in the band together a bit of a no-no in the near future.'

'Exactly.'

'Well not to worry.' Richard was casual. 'I'll talk to him and see if he minds if we carry on with Blake for a while.'

'Thanks. I'd appreciate it.' She paused. 'Erm. There's something else, too. Something I want to ask you about as a friend.' Frankie looked uncomfortable. Richard waited. Then she blurted it out. 'Richard, have you ever got a gay vibe off me?'

Richard laughed. 'No! What makes you ask that?'

'Well I've been seeing this girl as a friend. Woman actually. She's twenty-seven. She's a lesbian and I think she's interested in me.'

'Are you interested in her?'

'Oh, I don't know. I'm all confused.' Frankie bit her thumbnail. 'She's going back to Ireland in about ten days time so I need to sort out my head before then. Is it fair to keep Derek waiting when I have some sort of feeling for this woman?'

'What's her name?' asked Richard

'Indigo.'

'Cool name!'

'I know. So what do you think?'

'Only you know you feel, Frankie. Do you properly fancy her?'

'I think I do, yeah.'

'It's just as well this happened before you got married, if you think about it.'

'You're right.'

'You might be bisexual. No harm in finding out.'

'How do I find out?'

Richard laughed. 'Do you need me to draw you a diagram?'

*

Frankie was sitting quietly in her room above the music shop when Indigo arrived for her second guitar lesson. She had told Indigo not to bother bringing her new guitar in, because they had another model the same that she could practise on.

'How have you got on?' asked Frankie.

'Okay I think!'

Frankie had decided she was going to discuss the break with Derek with Indigo after the lesson and see if Indigo mentioned having feelings for her. The prospect of such a conversation made it hard for Frankie to concentrate on the lesson. But Indigo seemed oblivious and sat down and began strumming away, proud to show off what she could do.

'I'm fine with the C, G and A minor,' said Indigo cheerfully. 'It's just the F that's really hard.'

'Everyone finds F tricky at first,' Frankie reassured her. 'How is your chord changing coming on?' Indigo strummed three bars with the chords she found easy, doing some nice smooth chord changes in between. But she got stuck on the F and began muttering and trying to fold her fingers into position.

'Drop your wrist and keep your thumb from peeking over the top.' Frankie said coming round behind Indigo. She leaned over her pupil. Their heads were very close. The moment Frankie touched her hand, Indigo turned her head and kissed Frankie. It wasn't a little peck either, but a full sensuous kiss. It made Frankie's head spin and she clutched Indigo on the shoulder. But when they parted, Frankie completely panicked.

She stood upright and turned her back on Indigo. 'I think the lesson is over,' she said coldly. 'It's time for you to find another teacher. You needn't pay for today.'

Indigo stared at her back for a few moments. Then she put the guitar down and walked to the door. 'I'm sorry,' she said. Then she left, closing the door behind her.

*

Back at the flat, Indigo was distraught. She had assumed too much and now it was too late to go back and undo everything. She had acted on her feelings without giving the situation much rational thought and now she was paying the price. She had really upset Frankie, which was the last thing she wanted to do. She had lost her friendship too. It was all a disaster. She had made a real mess of things. It was time to go home.

She got out her netbook and booked a flight for that evening. Fortunately there was a seat available. She went through Paul's belongings, chose a few little mementos and packed the rest of her things. Then she sat down and began to write a letter to Frankie. Her tears flowed as she wrote. Pulling herself together, she went to the post office and posted it by registered post, so that it would be delivered tomorrow.

Indigo dropped the flat key into Mrs Pettigrew and told her to take what she wanted of the things left in Paul's flat.

'Well this is a strange business and quite out of order, I'm sure,' said Mrs Pettigrew, angrily. 'You said you were staying until the end of the month and would sort everything out.'

'I'm sorry,' replied Indigo. 'It's a family emergency; I have to go back today.' She didn't care what Mrs Pettigrew thought and put her out of her mind as soon as she was back in the flat. She gathered her bags together, along with the white guitar safely packed in her dad's guitar case. She stood for a moment, looking round the flat. Then her taxi arrived and she shut the door on the flat for the last time. She was headed for Liverpool Street Station and after that, Stanstead airport.

*

Frankie was working in the music shop the next day, which was a Friday. The shop was busy and she didn't have too much time to think. But on the bus home she began thinking about Indigo again. Her emotions were all over the place. But she knew she didn't really want to lose Indigo from her life. She kept going over the good times they had spent together. She had felt joy then, the like of which she had never felt in Derek's company.

She had received a text from Derek this morning saying he was sorry for losing his temper and could they talk? She tried now, to think about Derek and their future but Indigo simply dominated her thoughts.

'I've made a big mistake,' thought Frankie. 'I need to apologise and get her back in my life again.'

As she was walking into her flat, her neighbour, Meg approached her holding an envelope. 'I took this in today for you. It's a registered letter.'

Frankie thanked Meg and took the letter. She thought it might be from Derek, but when she looked at the address, it was a stranger's handwriting.

She put the kettle on, sat on the couch and opened the letter.

Dear Frankie,

I don't know how to begin to tell you how sorry I am for ruining our friendship. I should have respected the fact that you are still in a relationship. I had no right to do what I did. I have messed things up so badly now. I guess there is no way back.

Since I met you, I have felt truly happy inside, for the first time in a very long time. There is something very special about you, Frankie. You are an amazing person. You are beautiful inside and out.

I know I might be making things worse with this letter but I want to tell you the whole truth. It wasn't just a casual kiss for me. My feelings for you run very deep. I would go as far as to say I have fallen in love with you.

That day we went round the markets was one of the happiest of my life. When we were sitting on those scooters looking at the canal and you were talking, something happened to me inside. You've just filled my whole world up ever since I met you.

I have never met anyone as wonderful as you and I know I never will. You are everything I have ever wanted in a woman. I feel like we were made for each other and I guess my excitement in having found you just took over.

I've never been in love before. It's a powerful feeling. When I'm close to you I just want to touch you. That's what made me kiss you.

Even if you could overlook what I did, we could never be just friends, Frankie, because I feel too much.

I have to go. Away from London, from England and from you. I am booked on a flight to Ireland tonight. By the time you read this letter I will be back in my world, which will seem so sad without you.

Please think of me sometimes. Forgive the kiss, if you can and remember our friendship, which was a lovely thing. It isn't my place to say this but please don't marry Derek. I know you don't love him the way someone should when they are getting married.

You deserve someone really special and I hope you find that person. I hope that you find happiness. There is a video in my head and heart of you singing and playing the Moonchaser. I will keep it, always.

I am missing you like crazy already. It is hard to say goodbye so I will just say...

Thank you for everything.

All my love, always,

Indigo

Frankie's tears fell like rain and her hand trembled as she held the page. Indi had gone. She had gone because of her. She was already back in Ireland. No longer just down the road. No longer there to make plans together. She was hundreds of miles away, in another country across the sea.

The idea of life without Indi was unbearable. She had been like a beautiful fresh breeze that had blown in unexpectedly, making the world seem new. Indigo's smile had lit up her whole life and now the future just looked dark and bleak.

Frankie was still in shock at the news that Indi had gone. Indi had sounded so very sad in the letter. All Frankie wanted to do was to take away that sadness. To comfort her and reassure her that everything was going to be alright.

'I need to hear her voice again,' she said aloud and then reached for her mobile phone. Indigo had only phoned her once. But what day was it? Like an idiot she had not saved the number, but it would still be in her call history. She searched her memory. It was the day after the gig at the Royal Swan. She had a flier somewhere for that gig. She kept all sorts of mementoes of the band. It was the gig with Suzie Rootz. Frankie rifled through a drawer and found the flier. It had been the eleventh of September. So Indigo must have phoned her on the twelfth.

She quickly scrolled through her list of calls received until she got to the right date. There was only one call that wasn't from one of her listed contacts. It said, 'Number unavailable.'

So that was it. She had lost her.

Frankie had been sitting on the couch motionless for twenty minutes when the idea suddenly hit her, filling her with hope. The landlady! She might have a forwarding address.

Frankie knew that the flat was in Great Titchfield Street and she knew Indi's dad had been called Paul Keane. She rushed over to her laptop and fired it up, pacing impatiently as it went through its starting up routines. She found the online phonebook and there it was. The flat number. She had ordered a taxi within seconds.

It seemed to take forever for the taxi to come but soon Frankie was on her way to Paul's old flat. The door was open and a middle aged woman with a very cross expression was just inside, putting clothes into boxes which she then left by the door.

'Hi, I'm sorry to bother you. Is this Paul Keane's old flat?'

'Who are you?' demanded the woman.

'I'm a friend of Paul's daughter, Indigo. She left me a message that she has gone back to Ireland but forgot to leave me a forwarding address. Do you have it, by any chance?'

Please God, she thought-let her have the address.

'A fine lot those Keanes turned out to be,' said Mrs Pettigrew angrily. 'That daughter of his was here supposedly sorting out his things. Then she disappears leaving me to sort out the junk she doesn't want. I'm sick of being dragged into their goings on! But as it happens, no. She didn't leave an address. If you catch up with her you can tell her from me, "thanks for nothing!"'

Frankie's heart sank as she took her leave and called for another taxi. She felt utterly distraught and couldn't stop the tears, even though she was standing on a public street.

She was glad to get home. Once there, however she didn't even make a cup of tea. She was thinking about what she knew about Indigo. She lived with someone called Gillian, but that was no use as Frankie didn't know her last name. She worked in Galway in a bookshop and her boss's first name was Brian.

Frankie's mind was working through the options. How many bookshops were there in Galway? It would be easy enough to find out. She armed herself with a ream of paper and a pen ready to make a list. The laptop was still switched on and she typed in 'Galway Bookshops.' She could phone all the shops and ask for Indigo. But was that fair on her, given the very strong feelings she had expressed in the letter? No, the phone wasn't right for something like this.

'Well,' she said aloud. 'It looks like I'm going to Ireland.'

CHAPTER 8

It was time to leave for the Candyhorse gig at the Singing Kettle. Frankie had her red guitar ready in its case by the door. She stood at the window, watching for Richard's van.

She had decided that she had been far too reliant on Derek for transport lately. She could drive, but didn't own a car. She had quite a bit of money put by for her 'bottom drawer' and was now committed to buying herself a little van. It needn't be very new or in great condition. As long as it got her and her gear from A to B, she'd be happy. But today, Richard was going to be her driver.

They loaded Frankie's guitar and amp into the van and set off for the pub. Blake was still standing in on drums for Derek. As Richard drove, Frankie said, 'I've been thinking about everything and I've come to a decision.'

'About that girl?'

'Yeah. She went back to Ireland. We kind of had words, mainly because I'm so confused.' Frankie deliberately missed out the bit about the kiss during the guitar lesson.

'So, I'm getting myself some wheels and I'm heading for the ferry on Tuesday to try to sort things out with her.'

'You're following her over there?'

'Well, just for a few days.'

Richard smiled. 'Wow! You must be keen.'

There was a surprise waiting at the gig for Frankie. Derek was sitting at a table talking to Blake.

'Hello,' he smiled. 'I'm just checking out the young pretender to my drumming throne here!'

'How's your hand?'

'A lot better, thanks. I should be able to play again next week.'

Blake went to help Richard unload the van and Frankie sat down in his seat.

'Do you want a drink?' asked Derek in a friendly manner.

'No thanks,' replied Frankie. 'I'll have one after.'

'I'm glad I've caught you,' said Derek clearing his throat. 'I've done a lot of thinking lately and I've come up with a bit of a plan.'

'What plan is that?' asked Frankie, cautiously.

Derek sat up straighter and pushed his hair out of his eyes. 'I've told my parents that we don't want that house and that we're going to wait a while to get married. So I've asked them to scrap the wedding plans for now.'

'Good grief! How did they take that?' Frankie was astonished.

'Not great but it's our lives at the end of the day, isn't it?'

'Yes.'

'So I thought maybe we could live together for a while, if that's alright with you.' Derek's tone was humble. He was trying to please her, she could see that.

'We could get a flat somewhere near where you are living now. Just to rent. Somewhere we both like. What do you think?'

She appreciated the fact that he had gone into battle with his parents to accommodate her needs. She knew how much this would have cost him in terms of good relations with his mum and dad. After all, he had to face his father every day at work.

Frankie put a hand over his good hand and said 'Thank you Derek. I really appreciate it. I still need a little time to myself next week. But I'll definitely think over what you have said.' She was saved from having to say more.

'Frankie! Sound check!' Richard was calling her from the stage area.

'Knock 'em dead,' said Derek encouragingly as she took to the stage. But when she looked back his face looked sad and he cut a lonely figure, sitting by himself at the table.

*

After the gig, Frankie avoided the usual drinks with followers of the band and went home early. Derek had stayed to watch the whole performance but he was surprisingly understanding about her wanting to go home early and hadn't insisted on driving her there. He merely offered, and when she said she was getting a taxi he walked her to the door and kissed her goodbye.

Back at home Frankie was running over and over the same thoughts that had been occupying her mind since Thursday. Derek's big change of attitude should have been at the front of her thoughts but the question that kept going round and round was, 'Am I gay?'

The trouble was, she had nothing to compare her feelings to. How did it feel to be gay? Did she just have an unexplained attraction to Indi, like a sort of girlie crush?

'I don't know myself anymore,' she thought.

She had definitely bonded with Indi in a way she had never done with a woman before. But it felt so different to the way she felt for, well, Sarah from the band for example. She had only known Indi for a matter of about ten days, yet her feelings for her seemed to be overwhelming the feelings she had for her fiancé whom she had known for over a year.

Derek had looked a little bit lost in the Singing Kettle, and seeing him sitting there alone and trying to make things up to her had tugged on her heartstrings. But the feeling was something close to guilt, or even dare she say it, pity. She didn't feel joy when she set eyes on him. Not the same way Indi made her whole being light up.

Was it possible that meeting Indi had shown her what real attraction felt like and showed up her feelings for Derek as a pale substitute?

People didn't just decide that they were gay overnight, did they? All this thinking was giving her a headache. All she knew was that she had to make things right with Indi and repair their friendship. Anything after that was in the lap of the gods.

*

Frankie bought her van on Monday. It was quite old and a little battered in places but it would do the trick. She had never driven a diesel vehicle before but she soon got used to it. On Monday night she packed for Ireland. She wasn't taking much. She had booked a week off work but she needed to be back for the Candyhorse gig on Saturday.

On Tuesday morning she set off for Holyhead. She hadn't booked a ticket on the ferry but when she got there, there were seats to spare. The sea was a little rough. She tried to settle her stomach by eating a sandwich and having a cup of tea and she went on deck a couple of times to get some air. She watched from the deck as they came into dock. This was her first time in Ireland and she was quite excited.

She was happy to be on the road again and quickly navigated herself onto the orbital motorway, following the signs for the west. Galway city was busier than she expected, but driving round it she sensed that it was also compact. She selected a Bed and Breakfast place on the sea front. Her room was small with pink walls and white bed coverings. There was a kettle, so she made herself a welcome cup of tea and ate the shortbread that was there.

Frankie was too tired for a shower yet so she just got into bed and snuggled up, feeling warm and relaxed now she was close to where Indi worked and lived. She was soon fast asleep and did not dream.

*

The B & B proprietor was called Breege. She was about fifty five and talked constantly. Her non stop gabbling was a bit of an assault on the senses but Frankie loved her accent. She boasted that she had made the heavy soda bread Frankie was eating for breakfast. It was indeed lovely, but Frankie had to resist the urge to ask if she had churned the butter as well.

Breege chattered on about how busy she was and Frankie quit listening. She was making a plan in her head of how the day should go. She would park up in the city and get a street map from the tourist information centre. She had a list that she had printed off from her computer of Galway bookshops and she would tick them off as she went along. Galway was a university city, so there were a lot of bookshops.

She started at a shop near the tourist information centre. It was actually just across the road. It was a very odd feeling, walking in, and imagining she might bump into Indi at any moment. It made her stomach churn with nerves and excitement.

She went up to the counter and simply asked if Indigo Keane worked there. She wasn't sure if she should say 'Miss Keane,' but decided that was a little formal. The first few places she tried were big bookshops, but she also tried second hand ones too. Each time she entered a new shop, her stomach flipped anew.

At lunchtime she went to the nearest café to hand. She didn't want to waste time choosing somewhere. She wasn't all that hungry. She had two sausage rolls and a cup of tea. She delighted in listening to the Irish accents all around her. They reminded her of Indigo.

After lunch, it was back onto the streets for more legwork. Some of the streets were amazingly narrow and a lot of the buildings were very brightly coloured. Blue and yellow seemed to feature a lot. There were a lot of buskers but she did not spend time stopping to listen. She was very focussed and more than a little nervous.

By the end of the day her feet were tired and she was getting anxious that she had not found Indi yet. She decided that this shop, Heneghan's, would be her last port of call before she turned in for the night. It was a medium sized shop with new looking dark green paintwork. It had a very small seating area towards the back.

Frankie approached the dark haired man at the counter and asked the same question she had been asking all day. 'Does Indigo Keane work here?'

'She does, but it's her day off today. Can I take a message for her? The man had a smiling face.

Frankie's legs went a little weak and for a moment she considered sitting down in the reading and coffee area. 'I've found her,' she thought. 'Thank God.'

'Thank you. I'll pop back in tomorrow and see her. No message.' Frankie smiled back at the man and left the shop.

She felt as though she were gliding down the street as she made her way back to the van. 'One more day,' she thought to herself. 'Just one more day.'

*

It was raining on Thursday morning and the sky was very dark. Frankie filled herself up with more of Breege's soda bread and felt generous enough to comment favourably on the breakfast. She had only booked in for two days which had worked out quite nicely, because hopefully she would be staying somewhere nearer Indi's home tonight. The thought excited her. She booked out and set off for the City centre again, parking the van in almost exactly the same spot.

Walking into Heneghan's Bookshop, Frankie felt shy and unsure of herself. What if Indi was mad with her for coming over? Then she saw Indi, standing behind the counter, reading the back of a paperback and writing something down on a pad. Frankie walked right up to the counter before Indi looked up and saw her.

Indigo's eyes went wide with amazement and she just stared at Frankie, still holding the book in her left hand and the pen in her right hand. Frankie delved in her back pocket and produced something small which she held up between them both.

'You left this at my shop. I thought you might need it. So here I am.'

It was a deep blue tortoiseshell guitar plectrum, shaped like a teardrop.

Indigo slowly reached out as if to take the plectrum, but instead clasped both of Frankie's hands briefly in hers. Indigo's eyes were shining. She gazed at Frankie as if she couldn't believe she was real. At that moment, the man who Frankie had spoken to yesterday came in from the back.

'Did you find that number?' he called as he came through the door. And then to Frankie, a brief nod and, 'Hello again.'

Indigo quickly withdrew her hands. She cleared her throat and said to Frankie, 'There's a pub a few doors down called The Granary. I'll meet you in there in ten minutes. Okay?'

'Sure.' Frankie smiled, said goodbye to the man and left the shop.

The Granary was painted a deep red colour and it had a heavy dark green door. It had a large window with a low sill. In the window was a strangely sparse display of bottles of whiskey and brandy, and cans of Guinness. You couldn't really see beyond the window because the interior looked very dark.

She went in. Inside was indeed dark despite there being a lot of wall lights. There was a patterned carpet and a very long bar lined with barstools. There were many pictures on the wall of men carrying rowing boats, and people with rugged faces, none of them smiling. Mirrors were everywhere and the place smelled of beer.

Frankie ordered a Coke and sat down at a table. She deliberately picked one that was away from the drinkers up at the bar. It was over in the corner.

After a few minutes, Indigo came in.

'Hiya!' the barmaid called cheerfully.

'Hi Rhona,' Indigo replied. 'I'll just take a 7 Up, please.'

She carried her drink over to Frankie's table and sat down. 'Well, you certainly know how to surprise a girl,' she grinned, her composure regained now. 'My heart is after doing the Riverdance in my chest!'

Frankie couldn't stop smiling. 'It's so great to see you Indi.' Then she hesitated. 'Is everything alright with your boss? I mean, is it okay to be here?'

Indigo was casual. 'Brian? Oh he's fine. I've worked there for seven years and I can pretty much work flexitime whenever I like. How did you know where I worked?'

'I made a list of all the bookshops in Galway and I spent all day yesterday going into them asking if they had an Indigo Keane working there.'

Indigo was astonished. 'You didn't! Wait, you've been here since yesterday?'

'I arrived in Ireland on Tuesday actually.'

'Did you fly?'

'I came on the ferry. I bought a van before I left so I'm in that.'

'How long are you here for?'

'Not long, I'm afraid. I have to leave on Saturday morning to get back for the Candyhorse gig.'

Indigo smiled. 'You came all this way to return my plectrum?'

'I wanted to say sorry. For how I reacted last week. It was really stupid of me. Indi, I panicked.'

'It's okay, really Frankie.' There was silence for a few seconds. Then Indigo said, 'So, we've got two days! Where are you staying?'

'I stayed for two nights in a B & B on the seafront but I haven't booked anywhere for tonight yet.'

'That's perfect. You can stay at my place. We have plenty of space and I'd love to show you my little corner of the earth. Where's your van?'

'What about your car?'

'Gillian dropped me off this morning because she was in town all day. She was going to take me back too but I'll text her.'

'That's great. We can travel together then and you can navigate.'

'What are we waiting for? Let's get out of the city!'

It was amazing how quickly they were out of the city and on the long narrow straight roads west. Indigo had said the area she lived in was called Connemara and that her house was near the sea.

It felt wonderfully intimate to be travelling in the same vehicle together. Frankie felt like she was on an adventure. Indigo felt so pleased to be with Frankie again. The radio played as they drove along.

They came to a little row of shops and Indigo directed Frankie to turn left. Suddenly they were in the countryside. The road was bordered by dry stone walls on both sides. The landscape was rugged and barren but very beautiful in a wild sort of way. There were sheep in the fields but they were very small and shaggy with black legs and quite unlike any sheep Frankie had seen before. Trees were few and far between but there were bushes dividing some of the fields.

'Wow the fields are small here!' said Frankie. The houses got further and further apart as they drove on. There were very few two storey houses. To the right and left of the road, small lakes appeared with reeds around the edges. They saw ponies cropping grass and passed an occasional pair of cyclists in brightly coloured clothes.

'This is about as far as you can get from Great Titchfield Street!' laughed Frankie.

'Do you like it?' asked Indigo earnestly.

'I love it!' Frankie said, emphatically. 'I've never been anywhere before quite like this.'

The colours of the landscape were unique. It was a kind of faded green and bracken colour, mostly. The mountains were a lilac-grey.

'It looks so different depending on what time of year you're here,' said Indigo. In the spring there's yellow gorse everywhere. In June there's rhododendrons and later, lots of Fuchsia. It all grows wild.'

'Are those blackberries?' said Frankie, lifting a finger from the wheel and indicating the bushes that lined the road.

'Yes. If you go a bit further north they have this stuff called Gunnera. It's giant rhubarb. And when I say giant, it's like, ten feet across. It blocks the view of the road and they have to use diggers to dig it up. It's amazing looking.'

'I'd like to see that.'

'Well, we can go for a drive and see all that.' Frankie noticed that Indigo sounded bright and happy. She was glad to see her friend so upbeat.

They turned right into a village lined with colourful pubs. The sea was on their left now. As they came out of the village they began to wind their way along a pretty coastal road. The beaches were very quiet and there were tiny boats moored everywhere. Frankie wanted to stop and admire the view but she thought she ought to get Indigo home first. Indigo had wound the window down and there was an amazing smell of sea air. It wasn't raining any more. A lot of the houses dotted about had B & B signs on the front. At last, Indigo pointed to a house and said 'This is it!'

The house was painted a nice shade of grey and was a single storey building. Frankie pulled up outside and Indigo let them in with a key.

'It's great to see where you live,' said Frankie. 'I can't believe how quiet it is here! You are so lucky. I mean, I love the hustle and bustle of London but this is just so beautiful.'

'Like you,' thought Indigo, looking at Frankie as they went inside. 'Just like you.'

CHAPTER 9

Indigo made them both a cup of tea. Frankie took hers outside and sat on the bench in the front garden, facing the sea. Indigo changed out of her work clothes into jeans and a cotton jumper and then began making up the bed in the spare room.

'The seagulls here are massive!' said Frankie, looking over the beach as Indigo joined her outside. Indigo laughed and managed to resist the temptation to ruffle Frankie's hair.

'Oh, I brought you a present from London,' said Frankie suddenly getting up and going to the back of her van. It was a box about sixteen inches squared, wrapped up in electric blue gift paper, with a gold bow on the top.

'What is it?' said Indigo as they sat back down on the bench.

'Open it and see!'

Indigo tore off the paper, a big grin across her face and with her cheeks slightly flushed.

'Oh how gorgeous!'

Inside was a tiny amplifier, perfect in every detail. It even had corner protectors on and a real black metal grill. It looked really sturdy.

'You won't believe how loud it is. It runs on batteries so you can play anywhere. It's got all sorts of effects on the top and even a tuner. There's no excuse for you not to be the next Melissa Etheridge now!'

'You are so kind. I love it. Thank you, Frankie.' Indigo cradled the little amp on her lap and looked at Frankie. 'How are things with you and Derek?'

Frankie puffed out her cheeks and sighed heavily. 'He's turned over a new leaf. He's told his parents the wedding's off for the time being. He wants us to rent a flat in Camden together.'

Indigo did not make any reply. They stared at the sea for a while then Indi said softly, 'Why are you here, Frankie?'

The seagulls wheeled about and cried out as Frankie spoke.

'I know it must seem like I'm messing you about. The truth is, I am really confused, Indi. I thought I loved Derek. I thought I was happy to be on my way to becoming Mrs Doyle. Everything in my world was settled. That was until I met you and you turned everything upside down.'

Indigo spoke cautiously. 'So you do have some kind of feeling for me then?'

'I do. It feels very strong.'

'I'm so happy to hear that. I thought you were mad at me for what I did.'

'Not any more.'

'Well, you know how I feel about you, Frankie. I didn't hold back much in that letter.'

'Yes, I know.' There was another long silence. Then Frankie went on, 'Do you think I could be a lesbian, Indi?'

'Would it bother you if you were?'

'No. Not the way you mean. It's just that I don't know for sure. How can I have been happy with Derek if I was gay all along?'

'I'm not sure you were.'

'How do you mean?'

'I'm not sure you were happy with Derek all along. Let me put this amp inside and we'll take a walk on the beach.'

Frankie carried the cups in and rinsed them under the tap. Then the two women crossed the road and started to walk along the sand.

'I've never had a boyfriend,' said Indigo. 'I knew I was gay from puberty, really. But lots of gay women I know came out late in life. You are only twenty-three. I've known ones that came out at thirty-five. Or in their forties. I even heard the other day of a woman who came out at fifty one. It's my friend's older sister actually. She kept it to herself all this time. She was very unhappily married to a man she didn't love. She's so content now. I'm no wise-woman but I will say this. Don't get married if you have doubts about your sexuality. It will only end in heartbreak for the two of you. I'm not just saying that because I have a vested interest. I'm really not. I've seen it ruin lives too many times.'

'I know. And you're right.' They walked on for a while without talking.

Finally, Frankie said, 'Indi. Let's really try to enjoy these two days.'

'I'm really enjoying them already,' grinned Indi. 'No trying necessary!'

*

Indigo and Frankie grabbed a bite to eat back at the house.

'How do you fancy some *ceol agus craic* now?' Indigo asked.

'Some what?'

'It means "music and fun" in Irish. You'll love my local. They have trad music there on Thursdays, Fridays and Saturdays so we're in luck tonight.'

The two women strolled along to the pub from Indigo's house. It was called 'Canavan's' and was a whitewashed long low building with a thatched roof and turf smoke coming from the chimney. Inside there was a slate floor, and a bar with a wooden counter. There were lots of half poured pints of Guinness sitting on the drip trays behind the pumps.

'What's going on with the half filled glasses of Guinness?' whispered Frankie.

'He lets them settle and then tops them up.'

'You can't just pour them and serve them then?'

'No. There's an art to it. Are you ready for your own pint of the black stuff?'

'I most certainly am!'

Ten minutes later they were sitting at a table with a pint of Guinness each. Frankie said it tasted much nicer than it did at home.

'Yeah, they say it doesn't travel well.'

Frankie was amazed to hear most of the locals conversing in Irish. 'I never realised they actually spoke Irish nowadays,' she whispered to Indigo.

'Oh yes, especially in the Gaeltacht. That's what they call the designated Irish speaking areas. There are quite a few dotted around the country.'

'It sounds lovely, doesn't it? Can you speak any?'

'Of course. What would you like me to say?'

'Anything you like!'

Indi thought for a minute and then said, quietly, '*Tá tú súile álainn.*'

'What does that mean?'

'It means, "How are you?"'

'Cool. I'll try and remember that.'

At the table next to them, people with acoustic guitars, banjos, fiddles, accordions and tin whistles began to gather in a group. They all chattered noisily. It really was a lively pub.

*

Over in England, in the Singing Kettle, three quarters of the band, Candyhorse had gathered. They didn't have any instruments with them, however. Richard had called a band meeting.

'Is Frankie coming?' asked Derek, hopefully.

'No, mate. That's one of the reasons I called this meeting.' Richard looked round the table before making his announcement. 'Frankie has actually gone to Ireland.'

You could have knocked Derek down with a feather. 'Ireland? What for?'

'She's got a thing for a woman who lives there. She has been showing her round London, but now this woman has gone back, she's followed her over there.'

Sarah looked stunned too. She looked at Derek to gauge his reaction. His eyebrows were pulled down and his face was screwed up in disbelief.

'What do you mean, "A thing"?' Derek finally managed to say.

'This woman; she's called Indigo; is a lesbian. Frankie thinks she might be one too, because they've got close.'

'How do you know all this?' asked Sarah. Derek was still too stunned to say anything else.

'She told me,' said Richard simply. 'I know it's hard on you, mate,' he looked at Derek when he said this. 'But we need to know where this leaves the band. We've got Blake in on drums, who doesn't know where he stands and Frankie jaunting off round the world. It's all becoming a bit...' he searched for a word... 'Unstable.'

'I'm her fiancé and I was the last to know,' said Derek, miserably. 'It all falls into place now.' He rubbed his sore hand.

'She says she'll be back for the gig on Saturday but it's all going to be a bit awkward with you guys isn't it?' Richard meant Derek and Frankie. 'I mean, you're back playing this Saturday, aren't you Derek?'

'God, I never would have guessed that Frankie was a lesbian!' This from Sarah. 'It just goes to show; you never do know!'

'It's a shame Blake doesn't play rhythm guitar,' Derek said, bitterly. 'Then Frankie could stay in her love nest with the hippy woman and we'd have a proper band again.'

'Derek, you must be feeling terrible,' said Sarah, sympathetically, touching his arm.

'Oh, it's been coming for a while.' Derek was resigned to his fate. 'I just never guessed the lesbian part. I thought she was sneaking round with some bloke and using the Irish woman as cover.'

'Well, now you know, mate,' said Richard.

'I still care about the band,' said Derek, bravely. 'I want to go on playing in it but I don't think there's room for me *and* Frankie there. Do you guys agree?'

Richard took a gulp of his drink and looked round the table. 'I think Frankie's out guys. For good. We're going to have to cancel Saturday's gig and find ourselves another guitarist.'

'Who's going to tell her?' asked Sarah.

'Me,' said Richard brutally. 'I'll do it now. Are we all agreed?'

'Agreed,' said Derek and Sarah together.

Richard went out into the little beer garden and dialled Frankie's number.

*

In Canavan's, Frankie was laughing at a joke someone had just told when her mobile phone rang.

'Excuse me,' she said. She went out the front door of the pub and stood on the street. She saw it was Richard calling. Just what she didn't need... a reminder of home.

'Hi Richard,' she answered.

'Hi Frankie. How's your trip going?'

'Good thanks. Is anything wrong?'

'Yeah, kind of.' Richard's voice sounded a bit strange. 'The thing is, Frankie, we've had a band meeting and Derek feels he can't carry on with you in the band, given your situation. So, I'm sorry, but you've been voted out.'

'What? Derek doesn't know I'm over here or about what is happening. We're just on a break.'

'He knows now.'

'You told him?'

A pause. 'The band is important to me, Frankie. I can't just sit by and watch it fall apart.'

'How is Derek?'

'He's fine. He took it better than I expected actually. He really wants to get the band sorted too.'

'Well, thanks for wading in and organising my life for me.' Frankie was sarcastic now.

'Someone had to act, before the band just disintegrated. And if you want to know my opinion, Frankie, it was high time you put Derek out of his misery.'

'I see.'

'So. No need to rush back on Saturday now. There won't be a gig. We're going to advertise for a new guitarist straight away.'

'No flies on you, Richard.'

'Bye then, Frankie.'

'Goodbye.'

*

Sarah and Derek looked at Richard's face as he came back to the table.

'It's done,' he said, firmly. He went to the bar.

Derek looked helplessly at Sarah who unexpectedly took his hand.

'It'll be okay, Derek. Plenty more fish in the sea. And you've still got us.'

'Thanks, Sarah. You're very kind.'

'The truth is, I've always liked you, Derek.'

He looked into her face to see if he was picking up her meaning properly.

In reply, Sarah smiled a little smile, and nodded once.

*

Frankie put her phone back in her pocket and shivered. Indigo came out of the pub door and looked enquiringly at Frankie. 'What's wrong?'

Frankie sighed. 'I'm not sure where to start. Can we go back to your house? I can't face all the noise just now.'

'Sure.' Indigo took Frankie's arm and they strolled the short distance to Indigo's house. They did not speak as they walked back.

Gillian answered the door and greeted them warmly. Introductions were made and she made them all a cup of tea. The living room was cosy and lit only by candles placed in a row on top of the mantelpiece and the turf fire. Gillian chatted to Frankie for ten minutes and then said goodnight and went into her bedroom.

'You look a bit shook up,' said Indigo, when they were alone. Something's happened hasn't it?'

Frankie didn't say anything in reply. She just started to cry, big fat tears that rolled down her cheeks and dripped onto her lap.

'Oh Frankie!' Indigo was at her side instantly. Tentatively she put her arm around her friend. Frankie put her head on Indigo's shoulder and they sat like that for several minutes.

Then Frankie sat up straight and said, 'I'm sorry.'

'Don't be silly.' Indigo handed her a box of tissues and Frankie blew her nose and dried her eyes. 'We all have to let it out sometimes,' Indigo said. She made another cup of tea without asking and handed it to Frankie.

Frankie was composed now. 'That phone call was from Richard. He told Derek tonight that you and I have been seeing each other and that I'm over here.'

'Oh, God. How did he take it?'

'Quite well, apparently. He can't have been too devastated because they had a band meeting and they've voted me out.'

'Out of Candyhorse?'

'Yep'

'Oh no! That Richard had no right...' Indigo tailed off.

'A part of me is relieved, Indi.'

'So is it all over then, between you and Derek?'

'It looks that way.'

'This is all my fault, Frankie.' Indigo bit her nails. 'Since you've met me you've lost everything... your fiancé and your band. I've messed up everything for you.'

'No. Derek and I had to come to an end. And after all we've been to one another there's no way we could have carried on in Candyhorse. I'm free now. Free of him at last. I don't regret anything that's happened.'

'Are you going to phone him?'

'No I'll write to him. I'll do it now and send it by express post in the morning. Have you got paper and an envelope and a pen?'

'You're very brave.'

'I'm sorry I spoiled our night out.'

'We'll have plenty more. I'll leave you to write your letter. Just put the fire guard up when you've finished. Your bed is all ready.'

'Thanks Indigo. Goodnight.'

'Night.'

*

It didn't take Frankie long to write the letter. She sealed it, addressed it and propped it up on the kitchen worktop. Then she blew out the candles, put the fireguard up and went to bed.

Dear Derek,

I'm so sorry things have ended this way. Our time together was a very special time in my life, and I hope in yours. I hope we can both look back on all the good times and be glad we spent that year together.

You are a very lovely person and will make someone a great husband one day.

It wasn't to be... us as a couple for life but we had something good once and I'll always look back on that fondly.

I wish you every happiness in your life,

Love Frankie.

*

Frankie slept better than she expected she would. It had been a very long day and a very emotional one. In the morning, she awoke to see Indigo opening the curtains in her room. There was a cup of tea and a plate of toast by the bed on a little table.

'Morning, sleepyhead!'

'Morning.' Frankie smiled sleepily and stretched.

'You've been asleep for hours, it's half past eleven.'

'No! Oh God, my letter!'

'I posted it by express service first thing this morning,' said Indigo brightly. She sat on Frankie's bed.

'Thanks. You're very thoughtful.'

'How do you feel? Now you've written to him and had a sleep?'

'I feel good. Like this is a fresh new start for me.'

'I think it was for the best that you and Derek didn't get married.'

'Yes. It was.'

'You'll miss being in the band.'

'We could start our own girl band, "Indigo's Girls."'

Indigo laughed. 'That name sounds just a little bit too familiar.'

'Maybe we could call ourselves "Moonchaser".'

'I like the sound of that. But I have to learn how to play first.'

'We could have matching Moonchaser guitars. Do you think you'll ever get one now, or are you happy with the guitar you have?'

'I'm happy with it. You made a good choice.'

'Do you ever wonder what happened to your dad's guitar?'

Indigo smiled. 'I'm sure it's in safe hands with someone who loves it.'

CHAPTER 10

Indigo had left Frankie to shower and dress and now they sat side by side on the bench again, outside Indigo's house. It was a lovely autumn day with surprisingly warm sunshine.

'I hope I'm not assuming too much, but you won't be leaving tomorrow now after all, will you?'

'I'd like to stay on for a while. If you'll have me.'

'Stay as long as you like. Have you squared it with work?'

'I'll ring them today. It'll be fine.'

'That's good because I've made plans for us for today. And tomorrow.' Indigo was looking at the sea, but couldn't hide a small smile of pleasure.

'Oh, where are we going?' Frankie was curious.

'You'll need to pack an overnight bag with your wash things and night clothes.'

'Wow! Are you serious? We're staying away somewhere tonight?'

'Yep! We leave here at about half past two, in my car. You'll need to bring a little bit of spending money as well. Oh, and a warm jacket.'

'Well, you have me thoroughly intrigued now!'

Indigo smiled again. 'Shall we walk to the shop and get a paper? It's a nice day for a stroll.'

*

At two-thirty Frankie and Indigo were ready with their bags packed. They got into the car and began driving. They had only gone about five miles when Indigo slowed down and began to indicate.

'An airport?' said Frankie. 'Are we picking someone up?'

'Nope!' Indigo was really enjoying her surprise. 'I hope you don't mind flying Frankie, because we're going to be on a plane in just over an hour.'

'A plane?'

'Yes a real live plane with wings and everything,' Indigo laughed. 'You're very funny when you're in shock!'

'I haven't got my passport with me. Where are we going on a plane? I can't believe there's even an airport out here.'

'You won't need your passport. We're not going far. Have you ever heard of the Aran Islands?'

'No.' Frankie was still trying to get her head round the fact that they were going on a plane, today!

'There are three little Islands just off the coast and we are going to Inis Mór.'

'You're an amazing woman, Indigo Keane, How much is this costing you?'

'It's not expensive, so please don't give it another thought. We're only staying twenty-four hours.' Indigo parked the car and they got out. 'Our flight leaves at four. It's a dinky little plane, you'll love it. I've booked us in at a B & B which is also a Restaurant, so we can eat there tonight. We won't be able to explore much before dark this evening but we'll have most of tomorrow.'

'I can't believe we are going on a plane. This is mad!'

The interior of the airport was tiny, but with smartly green uniformed staff and all the usual fixtures and fittings. Indigo checked them in and then they were asked to step on a scale. Their weight was called out and printed on their tickets.

Frankie had a huge smile on her face. 'I've never been weighed for a flight before!'

When it was time to board they walked over to the little plane and a member of staff directed each of the seven passengers to particular seats. The largest passenger, a man, was told to sit at the back. Indigo and Frankie were not actually sitting together but in the small space they weren't far apart either.

Travelling down the runway, it felt like they were going very, very fast in a car with a lot of rattling parts. Then suddenly they were ascending into the sky.

Frankie had a good view of the pilot flying the plane. She kept turning round and grinning at Indigo, who grinned back. The passengers made jokes about what the in-flight movie was going to be and asked each other when the meal was being served.

It was quite a bumpy ride but before they knew it, they were landing. The sea looked tropical from the air and the sand on the beach looked very pure.

Inis Mór was an incredible looking island. Everywhere there were dry stone walls and tiny fields. It was rocky and quite flat in parts. There were horses and carts taking people around and lots of people on bicycles.

A minibus took them to where they were staying. It was a large traditional thatched seaside cottage which was built in the 1930s. As they got closer, they could see it looked like two long, low cottages pushed together.

Their room was small and cosy with very dark furniture and twin beds. There was exposed stone on one wall and heavy dark wooden beams elsewhere. The window was small but had a window seat. The bathroom was separate. The bed covers were purple and white patchwork.

They sat on their respective beds, each reading a leaflet about things to do and see on the island. The owner had told them dinner would be served at seven. They took a long walk on the beach before they ate.

Dinner was a delicious Irish stew. The dining room had whitewashed walls and a very dark wooden ceiling with sloping edges. There were simple wooden shelves on the walls, holding patterned plates. Some tables were oval and some rectangular. The seats were of an old fashioned wooden design with cushions tied on to make them more comfortable. There was an enormous fireplace at one end of the room.

Frankie and Indigo got their jackets from the room and set off on foot for one of the local pubs. Sitting with pints of Guinness, they listened to the musicians playing traditional Irish music. The man near to Frankie had a guitar. He was about sixty-five and was wearing a suit jacket and a cap. He said something to her in Irish.

'Tá tú súile álainn,' she replied, remembering perfectly the greeting from last night. The man looked at Frankie in amazement and then slapped his thigh and roared with laughter. Frankie looked at Indigo blankly. Indigo was hiding her face in her hands and shaking with laughter.

The penny dropped and Frankie whispered, 'Alright, you comedian. What did I just say to him?'

'You said he has very beautiful eyes!'

A woman with long dark hair began singing something in Irish without accompaniment and everyone stopped talking to listen. Frankie didn't understand what she was singing about, but it was a haunting melody. She looked at Indigo who was radiant and very fresh-faced looking after her walk to the pub. She wanted to put her arms round Indigo and kiss her. She was delighted to see Indigo looking so happy.

The sad song ended and a fiddle struck up a jaunty tune.

'This is really perfect,' said Frankie, simply to Indigo. 'Thank you.'

The night wore on and there were less people in the bar now. The man with the guitar had seen Frankie watching his hands as they shaped the chords. He instinctively knew she played and handed her the guitar.

Frankie was not shy about performing in public. She gave a perfect rendition of the U2 song, 'One.' Indigo was mesmerised. At the end everyone clapped and whooped.

They were quite merry as they left the pub together and walked back to their B & B. The moon was full.

In the room they undressed without looking at each other. Their beds were close together and each woman lay on her side facing the other.

'Indigo?'

'Yes?'

'Do I really have beautiful eyes?'

'Beautiful eyes, beautiful hair, a beautiful smile and most importantly a beautiful heart.'

'Your face was glowing in the pub,' said Frankie, softly. I've never seen you look so happy.'

'Every moment I spend with you is happy.'

'Indigo?'

'Yes?'

Frankie said no more. She simply raised the cover of her bed and moved over to one side.

Indigo left her own bed and lay down on the space Frankie had made. In each other's arms, they proved their love for one another until the sun came up.

*

The little cottage nestled on the lake shore, protected by the blue-grey mountains surrounding the water. It was the following summer. The evening was hot and balmy. Dragonflies of green, brown, blue and red zipped about above the surface of the lake. The water was very still and held a perfect reflection of the mountains and the sun which was very low in the sky and was coloured deep orange.

The two women came out of their home hand in hand, walked to the water's edge and spread a blanket on the earth. One was carrying a dark brown guitar with brilliant white moons adorning the fret board.

They sat close together on the blanket and kissed, their fingers entwined.

'I've never played you any Buddy Holly songs, have I?' said Frankie, pulling the Moonchaser onto her knee.

'No, you never have,' replied Indigo, softly.

'Do you know this one?' Frankie began to strum and sing as Indigo looked out across the lake.

Sometimes we'll sigh
Sometimes we'll cry
And we'll know why
Just you and I
Know true love ways

Indigo's eyes filled with happy tears as a heron flew overhead and the sun touched the water, flooding the surface with colour.

THE END

"True love ways" written by Buddy Holly &
Norman Petty

Contact Rain McAlistair at:

rainmcalistair@eircom.net

Printed in Great Britain
by Amazon

58059258R00071